One Thousand and One Days

Renee Frey

AUTHORS 4 AUTHORS PUBLISHING
Marysville, WA, USA

Published by Authors 4 Authors Publishing
1214 6th St
Marysville, WA 98270
www.authors4authorspublishing.com

Library of Congress Control Number: 2020942648

E-book ISBN: 978-1-64477-067-2
Paperback ISBN: 978-1-64477-068-9
Audiobook ISBN: 978-1-64477-069-6

Edited by Rebecca Mikkelson
Copyedited by Brandi Spencer

Cover design and illustration ©2020 Christina Myrvold. All rights reserved. Interior design by Brandi Spencer

Authors 4 Authors Publishing branding is set in Bavire. Titles set in Gondola. Handwriting set in Redressed. All other text is set in Garamond.

One Thousand and One Days

Renee Frey

Authors 4 Authors Content Rating

This title has been rated 17+, appropriate for older teens adults, and contains:

- Brief sex
- Moderate language
- Moderate violence

Please, keep the following in mind when using our rating system:

1. A content rating is not a measure of quality.

Great stories can be found for every audience. One book with many content warnings and another with none at all may be of equal depth and sophistication. Our ratings can work both ways: to avoid content or to find it.

2. Ratings are merely a tool.

For our young adult (YA) and children's titles, age ratings are generalized suggestions. For parents, our descriptive ratings can help you make informed decisions, but at the end of the day, only you know what kinds of content are appropriate for your individual child. This is why we provide details in addition to the general age rating.

For more information on our rating system, please, visit our Content Guide at: www.authors4authorspublishing.com/books/ratings

Dedication

To my dearest Mike,
who first gave me the push to sit down and write.

Table of Contents

Prologue

Day 1001: Sutaita

It has been one thousand and one nights since I was supposed to die.

This is my one thousand and first day as wife to the Emperor Shahryar, Sultan of all Persia.

Opening my eyes and stretching on our shared gilt canopy bed, I glance over and see him snoring softly in the dawn light. I cannot help but smile at his beautiful face. I cannot help but admire this man, in spite of the horror I've witnessed first hand. In the past thousand days, he has grown from an impetuous youth into a true sultan, a leader who will leave his mark on history and the world. But his success cannot make me happy.

I am out of stories. Out of time. Today, I will meet my fate. This morning, my husband will kill me. I will become nothing more than a name.

But I will be free.

One Thousand and One Days

Chapter 1
Day 0: Sutaita

I returned home from my daily studies to find my father in the small niche of our home reserved for prayers, prostrate on his prayer rug, weeping. I glanced around, searching for my younger sister. The cooking area was tidy, gleaming pots sitting empty on the stone counter, the fire in the hearth banked. Dunyazade was not here. Dunyazade would know what to do. She always knew how to help when someone was overcome with emotion. I fought down the nervousness I always felt when others displayed their emotions. Biting my lip, I stood silently, unable to act. My indecision would not help my father—but there was nothing I could think of that would.

After a moment, I washed my hands, feet, and face in the basin next to the niche, pouring water from the ewer as needed to complete the wudu, the ritual cleansing before prayer. I crossed the room, pulled out my prayer rug, and laid it slightly behind his. Our prayer room, simple and austere, usually gave me peace. A warm breeze flowed through the window, making the linen curtain dance. The smell of honey, basil, and frankincense from the market filled the niche. It was no match for the heavy cloud hanging over my father. The unadorned stone walls and clean wooden floor echoed his grief. I knelt down, facing Mecca, and silently began saying my prayers. Allah, who knew all men's hearts, would inspire me. Through Him, I might help my father.

Prayers concluded, my father stood, rolling up his prayer rug. I did the same, watching sumptuous red and gold cloth disappear into itself. Father gently took my rug from me and placed it on the rack next to his own, but his eyes were glazed over as if he wasn't really there. Turning my head, I avoided meeting his eyes. My nerves jangled with discomfort. I followed him out of the praying niche and into the main room of our house. He turned to me, grief shadowing his entire countenance. I swallowed nervously but met his gaze. My father needed me; nothing else mattered.

"My Scheherazade..." His nickname for me made me smile, uplifting my concern for the moment. Freedom, he called me. As his oldest daughter,

3

I never understood how I could represent freedom to him—but freedom he called me, nonetheless.

My smile broke what little control he had. He pulled me into his arms, crushing me in a tight hug. I returned his embrace, despite my own unease and my general dislike of physical touch. The faint aroma of tea and cloves enveloped me—his scent was still unchanged, even after all these years.

After recovering, my father drew back and met my eyes. "I have no choice."

"No choice in what?" Despite the tightness in my throat, I spoke clearly.

"The decree...the maidens...I cannot find any more."

My heart beat faster. "The sultan?"

"He requires another wife. And there are no more eligible maidens in the city—save yourself and Dunyazade."

My eyes dropped to the ground. "I see." For the past half year, the Sultan of Persia had decreed he would marry a new wife each evening and murder her on the following day. Father would have to sacrifice one of us to the sultan. Either my sister or I would be dead the following morning.

For a moment, it seemed as though time stood still. Part of me didn't quite believe what my father said. I hadn't concerned myself with the sultan's decree, had assumed my father's rank in court would keep me safe. I should have known better. Many other high-ranking women were already dead. A heavy pit descended in my stomach.

My father strode into our parlor, his soft brown eyes glistening with unshed tears. I knew, deep within, he would never offer either of his daughters to the headsman's block. Family was the most important thing to him. I also recalled how, for the past few weeks, he had been away more and more as he traveled great distances to procure the brides the sultan demanded. And now, he was out of options.

I approached him, laying a hand on his arm. "You are Ja'far, the Chief Vizier. You have the ear of the sultan. His vow to kill each bride the morning after the wedding is the very height of folly. How will he conceive an heir? What of the Empire when he dies?"

My father shook his head. "Do you think I have not tried? Every day as I took another daughter from her parents, I attempted to persuade him. There is no argument, no line of reason I have not presented. He does not care—his rage is too far gone. He has no heir, and will not unless he keeps a wife at least long enough to bear a child. Unless he will raise a bastard like himself to the throne."

He walked over to the assortment of cushions along the wall and sank down into them. "I thought, with time, the right girl would convince him. But despite the bloodshed, he holds true to his edict." He buried his face into crossed arms.

Rather than respond, I strode over to the open window, staring at everything and nothing. The crowded streets of Baghdad made no impression on my inner turmoil. The sultan was a problem. What would he do two days hence when there were no more maids to wed and slay? Logically, something would have to change. Could I change it? Could I tease out a solution? Despite every racing heartbeat warning me against it, the puzzle presented by the sultan intrigued me. The man was intelligent, surely, or he'd not have kept his empire through several trials and battles, including the recent civil unrest and the war with Byzantium. Which meant this holdup was something else. Something emotional. Something I didn't understand. Could I learn enough about him and his emotions to stave off execution?

Thinking of the dozens of brides he'd already slaughtered sent a shudder through my spine. No wonder Father's logic hadn't worked. The man must be mad. Then I thought of what would happen if Dunyazade were his next bride, and my blood turned cold. Father would be forced to watch—as, in all likelihood, would I.

There had to be a way out of this. And if not...

Despite my clammy palms and nausea, resolve overcame me. I could not stand by and watch my only sister be murdered.

I thought of the future I had planned for myself—a life of study and solitude, quiet contemplation and education. The towering spiral of the House of Wisdom caught my eye. My heart sank. Done were my days of learning there. This was probably my last day alive. But for me, there was no other way.

"I will do it," I said calmly, my voice belying the sinking feeling in my stomach that I felt at my decision. What hubris had I, to believe I could solve an impossible challenge, one based on emotions, my biggest weakness, in one night? Every physical part of me railed against it, demanded that I run, hide, do anything besides consign myself to this fate.

"What?" My father lifted his head, face ashen.

"I will marry the sultan. But if it is to be tonight, per his decree, I must find my sister and make preparations."

Too many emotions crossed my father's face for me to decipher. He had already lost his wife—and now he was doomed to lose both daughters. He started to speak, but seemed to realize that words could not possibly express the depth and range of his feelings.

"No." He finally forced the word out. "I refuse." His voice boomed as he tried to overpower me with sheer force of will. "I will not allow it, Sutaita."

His eyes met mine. I gazed back at him without uttering a sound. Rather than engage in an argument, I waited. Once he exhausted his reasoning, I knew I could convince him. His gaze steeled, brown eyes becoming hard.

"I will not sacrifice you for him. You are my—"

"I am the best chance you have to save Dunyazade."

My well-chosen words resounded through the room. When my father's eyes dropped to the floor, I knew then that I had hit the mark. While I loved my father, and he loved me, Dunyazade was the image and spirit of my late mother. Losing her would destroy him. Losing her would decimate me. When I saw his shoulders slump down in resignation, my victory was assured.

"This choice is my choice—to save my dear sister. If I am freedom, let me free her as well as you. Let me do this."

When he finally looked at me again, his eyes filled with sorrow, but he turned toward the door. "I will make your intentions known to the sultan." With that, he departed the house.

For a moment, I couldn't move, couldn't breathe. What had I just agreed to? I fought the trembling feeling washing through my limbs. This was it—this was how I would die. My eyes glistened with tears as the enormity of what I'd undertaken took hold of me. This was not a puzzle based on numbers and facts. This was a scavenger hunt for some mysterious happening that caused an emotional reaction. And I'd have mere hours to search. I'd doomed myself.

I began to plan my wedding-funeral.

Dunyazade found me sitting in the bathing room, staring blankly at a washing cloth. I glanced over when I heard her approach. Her eyes were wide with fear—fear that I would die, fear that she would die soon after. I did my best to stay calm, but I must confess that I was more afraid than I had ever been in all my life. Even after years of civil war tore my country apart, even after losing my mother, even when I learned of the truly evil capacities of men during my quest for knowledge and wisdom, I was never more afraid than I was now. I felt frozen, unable to move, unable to even think.

"I wish it were me instead of you." My sister's soft voice broke my reverie. "I should be marrying—you never wanted to marry, never wanted to be taken from your studies."

I cupped her face with my hands. I was her older sister. No matter my feelings, I must tend to her first. I shook my head. "No. It must be me. This we both know."

She hugged me tightly. "I wish there were something we could do."

I stayed in her embrace, tears flowing. My last night on earth, and I wouldn't even be able to spend it with my family. I would be in the company of a madman set on killing me for no crime other than my sex. My accomplishments, my learning, my dreams...all for naught. My sister sobbed as well. We were so close, especially since our mother died.

"What will I do without you? I can't lose you too!" Duny cried out.

Her sorrow beat at my already aching heart. I pulled away from the hug and brushed a tear off Duny's face. This problem, I could solve. "Remember the day that Mother—"

"I remember," she whispered.

I had been barely nine years old, still a child. She was but seven. We shared a room in a much smaller house—my father was not yet a vizier. The old sultan, Harun al-Rashid, still ruled.

"You told me the story," she continued.

"I did." Remembering that morning—it still made my chest hurt. Mother had just died. It felt like one moment she had been there, teaching us and guiding us, and the next, she was gone—sleeping but unable to awaken.

Duny shivered and sat next to me. "Sutai, I wanted to pretend that it was all a bad dream."

"I wanted to pretend too. I still miss her, even ten years later."

Duny laughed through her tears. "But you didn't. Instead, you told me a story."

I smiled in spite of myself.

"Tell it again."

So while Duny wet the cloth and began the ritualistic cleansing, I told her the parable.

"Once upon a time, there lived a fish—a fish who was in love with the forest. Every day she would swim as hard and fast as she could and flick her tail to launch herself into the air. She tried to fly out of her tiny pond and into the vast, beautiful forest. But every day, no matter how hard she swam, how strongly her tail flicked, she always fell back into her pond.

"One day, instead of trying on her own, the fish remembered the edicts of the Prophet and, instead, prayed to Allah. She prayed that Allah would allow her to meet the forest and its denizens, to be able to leave the pond that had become a prison, and to see and belong to another world.

"Allah is great, and the fish's prayers were answered. The sky darkened with clouds, and the rains came. It rained for a month and a day. The little pond swelled with water and turned into a lake, swallowing the forest inside of it. And the little fish knew joy, for she swam into the forest and explored.

"But the forest and its denizens cried with a sorrow deeper than words. The fish heard their wailing, felt their trembling, and finally asked what the reason was for their grief. Her new friends replied that they were starving. The lake had eaten all their food, and without sustenance, they would soon perish. The fish too knew sorrow in her heart, for she realized that in her selfishness, she had condemned the world she admired to death.

"The fish again prayed to Allah. She said, 'Allah, who is so great, so great that You have shown me life beyond my pond, please have mercy on me and my companions. Please restore the pond and the forest to the way You in Your Wisdom ordered them. I will be content to live life in my pond in order for my friends to live.'

"And Allah, who is great and merciful, shrank the lake back into the pond. The fish lived the remainder of her life content and never sought to alter reality for her own satisfaction."

A calm overcame me as I told the story. My racing heart slowed, and warmth flowed to my bereft limbs. That parable in particular centered me, brought the world into focus. Of course, I had to do this. I faced challenges head-on. I didn't run from them. I was who I was, and would be myself to the end. If I could solve this problem, I would do my nation a great service. And if I couldn't, I would end my days as they had begun, walking the path Allah set before me without hesitation or regret.

Duny gave one last strand of hair a pat before carefully pinning a flowing veil over it. "There. You look breathtaking."

I missed her already. If only I could tell her one last story, share one last moment. I wanted to curse the sultan for his ridiculous edict. How dare he be the fish of the story, who sought to impose his will on the world with no thought of the consequences for others? I thought of all the time I had spent at the House of Wisdom, reading and learning everything I could get my hands on. Now I would never be able to read another philosophy, never learn a new mathematical theory, never share my beloved knowledge with my even more beloved sister.

"Sutaita, thank you for the story. It will be something I can recall. A way I can remember to keep me strong tomorrow when..." Sobs overcame her.

For myself, I returned to the sense of purpose and comfort I found in telling the story. If I dwelt on tomorrow, I would only fall apart again. I felt as though I was detaching from the world, pulling away from my very humanity. Emotions would only remind me of my terrible fate.

One last story.

It was then that a brilliant idea occurred to me.

"Duny! I have an idea."

She looked up. "An idea for what?"

"I know how to beat him—how to survive." *How to save you.*

Duny frowned. "Sutai, I know you're clever, but don't you think the other girls have tried? What could you possibly do?"

I drew myself up. "I have read the Greek tragedies, the Egyptian myths, the epics of India. I know enough stories and fantastical happenings that I will tempt him with the most succulent fruit I know of—the ending of a story."

Duny gaped at me. "You think a story will save your life?" She shook her head. "Oh, Sutai..."

"No, it will," I insisted. "I won't ever finish the story at night. I will end with suspense and mystery, and leave him wondering what will happen next. He will stay his hand, telling himself that it is just one more night. And I will do that until..."

"Until when? Honestly, Sutai, how long can you keep that up for? A month? Maybe two?"

I thrust my chin out stubbornly. "I will do it as long as necessary. Until I find a way out of this."

Duny picked up a brush and a pot of cosmetics and began painting color on my face. "Sutai, it's a noble plan, but it won't work. Are you going to just start reciting the quests of Sinbad? Please."

"No...you're right, I can't just launch into it..." I snapped my fingers. "I've got it!"

Dunyazade stopped. Her eyes narrowed in suspicion. "Got what, exactly?"

"I will send for you. You will ask me to tell the story."

"The story of Sinbad?" She raised an eyebrow, fighting the amusement she knew was etched upon her face. "Sutai, this has got to be the craziest idea you've ever had. I don't want to lose you, but this won't work. This screams of desperation."

"It might not work, but it's the best chance we've got! Please, say you'll do it. And don't ask about Sinbad; ask for the story of the Trader and the Jinni!"

Duny regarded me with considering eyes. "All right." She rolled her eyes, no doubt resigned to join me in my crazy scheme. "But how are you going to sneak me in? I can't ask if I'm not there."

I stood up and paced. That was a problem I had forgotten. The sultan would more than likely be focused on claiming his spousal right. The thought of any man—that animal especially—touching me made my stomach roil.

"I will ask that you attend me. He is honor-bound to allow me one last wish before death."

Duny just stared at me. "You think he has honor?"

"He did—he does—he must. He won the war. He was chosen by his father to rule." I stood and gazed out the window, seeing the palace in the distance. "Somewhere inside him is a good and honorable man, representing the Prophet and leading us." I turned and smiled at Duny. "I just have to help him find it."

"Oh, Sutai." Duny blew out a breath, exasperated. She understood people well enough to know that, for men like the sultan, once pride was involved, there was no stepping down. "Remember the stories of the Greeks...and their hubris."

There was that word again. Maybe Dunyazade was right. Maybe this was my foolish pride, and I would make a fool of myself in the end. And yet, something beat at me from within, some spark refused to die. Despite how unlikely and insane this scheme seemed, all my learning, all my experiences, seemed to point to this as the best solution. And if I was truly honest with myself, the only solution.

Dunyazade walked over and finished with my face, then rearranged the veil to drape over it. "You look like a queen."

"You will come when I ask?" My eyes searched hers, asking a thousand times.

"I will come, Sister."

I looked in the mirror, a family heirloom that was to be laid out as part of the wedding spread, or the sofreyé aghd. My features were too strong to be considered beautiful. For so long, that had been an advantage for me. Dunyazade had taken after our mother, with almond-shaped eyes framed with dark, becoming lashes. My nose was far too prominent. But Duny had done her work well, using cosmetics to soften the harsh angles of my face and heighten the depths of my eyes. I hugged her one last time before we both left the room.

The ceremony concluded, guards escorted me to the royal wing of the palace. Maids came to make me ready to greet my husband. My husband. I was only nineteen years old. I knew that many girls had been married for years at my age. I felt so unprepared for this.

I had no mother to prepare or instruct me in the ways of being a wife. I cared not, since I had not planned on marrying. My father, a rarity of fathers, had accepted my scholarly leanings and not pushed me. He treasured my uniqueness. I think one reason I did not want marriage was because, deep down, I believed that there would never be a man who would value me as much as my father did.

The maids removed the elaborate brocaded wedding finery, replacing it with light golden silks and linens. My hijab was removed, my long black hair artfully arranged to drape about my face and shoulders. Their ministrations complete, the maids departed, and I was alone in the chamber. An enormous curtained bed awaited me. Plush cushions were strewn about the room. I looked at the bed, then at a cushion by the wall. I walked past the bed to the cushion and reclined on it. Much safer here.

The moon shone in through the window. I looked out over the city of Baghdad, wishing that I were a bird winging free through the night, instead of what I was—a scholar, a woman, destined to die in the morning. I remembered the fish story I had told my sister and bit my lip. Such wishing never wrought well. Footsteps alerted me to the sultan's presence. I knelt, head down, pulse racing.

"Rise." His voice was clipped and harsh.

I did as commanded, careful to keep my eyes down. He stalked around me, and I felt his gaze like a hot poker, stabbing and burning me everywhere it touched. I tried meditating, focusing on my breath. I must control my emotions.

The circling stopped. We both waited there in silence. After what seemed like an eternity, he grunted.

"Any last requests?"

Some of the tension drained from my shoulders. Despite his barbarism, he would honor the conventions and allow me one last wish before my death. I carefully spoke the request I had planned and rehearsed all afternoon. It took everything I had not to let a tremble escape on my voice, not to sob through my words.

"My lord, on this, my wedding night, I must admit I am frightened. I have no living mother to advise me. If I might summon my sister, that she support me and aid me, sparing you from my troubling, naïve maiden emotions."

I peeked at his face out of the corner of my eye. He looked confused. Had he expected blubbering? A plea for clemency? Of course he had. But I was not so foolish as to believe that a man inured to decency enough to slay dozens of brides would be diverted by melodramatic cries.

"Of course." His tone was still short and clipped, but puzzlement crept into it as well. Something about his discomfiture spoke to me, sang to me. Did he share my love of solving problems, of finding truth? Did my atypical response intrigue him the way his one inconstancy from logic and reason intrigued me?

He summoned a guard and ordered him to fetch my sister. Summons sent, Dunyazade appeared moments later. The mirror from the sofreyé aghd reflected her face behind me. She caught my eye, and I nodded ever so slightly.

"Dear sister!" She opened her arms.

I rose and approached her. "Dearest sister."

We both embraced, the sultan looking on with a curl of derision on his mouth.

"I will exc—"

"Oh, no!" Dunyazade jerked away from me to clasp her hands pleadingly. "Your Majesty, I will be here tomorrow eve—and bereft of a sister to comfort me! Please, stay—let us all enjoy the company of each other for just a moment. It will help ease my sorrow on the following eve." Her lips curved in a dazzling smile, brown eyes sparkling. I knew I could count on Dunyazade to do what I could not: to surprise, to attract, to redirect the sultan's anger.

The sultan looked positively confused. I surmised that his general disdain of females meant that he was completely unused to the maneuvering of women. I could not help but grin to myself. *Maybe this will work after all!*

Shrugging, he flopped down on the bed, making himself comfortable.

It was then that Dunyazade followed through with our plan. She asked me to regale her once more with her favorite story...

One Thousand and One Days

Chapter 2
Day 1: Sutaita

I spoke the words of the story until the gentle warmth of dawn peeked through the window. The trader was about to slay his son, who was transfigured as a calf. The sultan no longer lounged upon the mattress. Instead, he sat on the edge, leaning forward, eyes wide with anticipation. He looked almost approachable then, like someone who could be my friend, someone to laugh with, mayhap even cry with. Looking at his face, engaged in the story, emotion spilling through his soft brown irises, I felt something clutch in my chest that I'd never felt before.

"My lord,"—I lowered my eyes—"I fear I have spoken through the night. Look." I gestured toward the window.

The sultan frowned when the recitation stopped. His head whipped up, his eyes narrowing at the window. Sure enough, the deep black of night was lightening to the azure of dawn. His whole body tensed. He turned to me, eying me up and down.

My sister excused herself quietly and departed.

For the first time since being married, we were truly alone together. My pulse hammering, I tried to keep my face smooth. *Please let this work.*

He took one deep breath and then another. He approached me and clasped my face in his hands—rougher than I would have desired, but without harming me. His eyes bored into mine, delving into my soul. I tried to return his fiery gaze with equal depth of passion, but alas, I am not a fighter. I could only stare back and pray to Allah that my calmness gave him peace.

After a moment passed, seeming an eternity, he released my face. Not speaking a word, he bade me follow him by gesturing as he left the chamber. His loose white pants swished angrily. Taking a deep breath to calm the pounding in my own veins, I lifted my chin with confidence I did not feel and followed as gracefully as I could.

Just outside our chamber, the hallway split. He stopped and turned to face me again. "I do not know if this is trickery or wisdom." He paused, and thoughts of being dragged before the headsman flashed through my head, followed by an icy rush through my veins. "But you have bought yourself one additional night. Prepare yourself for the morning prayer." His eyes lit up with malevolence. "You will pray it with me." He turned to the right and continued stalking off.

My shoulders collapsed, and my knees gave out. I fought the desperate tears that threatened to overtake me. *One more night.*

I do not know how long I sat there, but a maid found me and urged me down the hall to the left. "My lady," she whispered, "he is certainly in a mood this morning. Come, let me dress you."

I followed her, the numbness of the previous day taking hold of me again. One night. I only had to survive today.

The maid *tsk*ed at my hair, then brushed and arranged it before undressing me. "I am, um, surprised that you are still wearing these."

I looked at her. She shook out the elegant nightdress, then began to fold it carefully. Did I need to tell her? *Maid, since I don't know your name, I regret to inform you that I spent my wedding night talking. Apparently, it was a wise investment of my time, since I will live to sleep at least one additional night.* Inwardly, I groaned. The words sounded so false, even in my own mind. Just because my scheme worked last night was no guarantee it would work again, or even continue to work long enough for me to accomplish my true aim: solving the puzzle of the sultan. There was no way to have this conversation with anyone—not even Dunyazade. Part of me was surprised I'd won even this one additional night. That instinctual push, that spark I'd felt yesterday, however, assured me that I was on the right path.

"Here, wear these for today." The richest garments I had ever seen laid across her outstretched arms. Flowing fabric sparkling with expensive metals and stones was pulled over me, whispering as it draped across my body and skimmed the floor.

I hated it. I was not a figurine to be dressed up and displayed. The garment, while beautiful, was impractical and uncomfortable. I attempted to hide my distaste, at least until the maid was no longer in the chamber. It wasn't her fault the gown was inappropriate and ostentatious.

Fully dressed, I followed the maid down the hallway toward what I presumed was the prayer niche. The simplicity of the space took me off guard. Compared to the rest of the palace, this room was austere. Cloth-of-gold drapes graced the windows, and the flicker of lit golden lamps danced through the room, but there were no tapestries, no rugs, no statues or vases. With closer inspection, I could tell the floors and walls were cleaned and cared for with the utmost attention. The mihrab itself was a beautiful blue and green mosaic with a hadith quote for blessing and peace inlaid in white and black tiling around the edge. My prayer rug sat next to the mihrab on the rack. I had not packed it, hoping it would remain with my family after my execution. I reached for it.

"Your sister brought it last night." The sultan's voice was cold and emotionless. "That was why she was able to attend us so quickly. She said you forgot it."

I looked over at him. Like me, he was attired in luxurious fabric, although the precious stones and metals on his robe were larger than mine. His eyes homed in on me, studying me, as if looking for fault or measuring me against some ideal. A thousand responses flitted through my head. I could tell him now how I duped him—used the power of a story to convince him to keep me alive. I could toss my head and refuse to care about my faults, real or imagined. I could explain how I wanted my prayer rug—an ancient family relic—to remain with my family, and thus chose to leave it behind. In the end, I elected to remain silent. It would serve me best to speak only when I told him stories.

While kneeling and silently echoing the words my husband spoke—it felt so odd to call him such—I tried to release my fears and concerns and find the calm center I'd discovered just the day before. My success this time, however, was not evident. My hands were again cold and clammy, and my stomach had tied itself in knots.

When we finished praying, I stood, waiting for directions from my husband. He remained on his prayer rug for many moments. I wondered what he was doing, but didn't dare interrupt him. Finally, he rose and gestured to a pair of guards waiting in the hall. They approached as he jerked my prayer rug from my fingers. Despite my best efforts, shock at his callous treatment must have shown on my face. It was just a prayer rug, but still.

All I could think of was why I hadn't brought it along in the first place. It was a gift from my late mother and had been handed down her family for generations. And he tossed it aside like nothing more than a piece of carpet. *Which is all it probably is to him. All I will ever be to him.* My eyes stung as tears filled them.

A fleeting expression of regret crossed his face, instantly replaced by anger. "There is a personal chamber prepared for you. You are to wait there for me. The guards will escort you there." He turned to leave.

"Pardon me, my lord...might my sister visit me?"

He whirled around. He seemed to hesitate, then muttered, "Fine. Send word to her. But you are not to leave the room, understand?"

I nodded and bowed in silent acquiescence.

Another guard trotted up and asked what message I would have sent to my sister.

I bit my lip, hesitating. "Ask her to bring my study materials and attend me as soon as she can—please."

The guard bowed—which surprised me—and departed.

Another of the guards caught the surprised expression on my face and chuckled. "You are a sultana now, yes? Maybe not as powerful as the Empress Irene of Athens, but you can command."

I looked at him. Part of me wanted to smile and share the joke with him. But I could not. Until I knew exactly what had caused a murderous rage that simmered in the Sultan for weeks, I could not afford to risk any behavior that would show me as indecorous or improper. I kept my expression blank. The guard shifted uncomfortably under my unwavering gaze before taking the lead down the corridor toward what I assumed was my personal chamber.

The room was opulently decorated with silk, gold, and linen furnishings. A small brazier burned a light jasmine-scented incense. Wide windows overlooked the gardens below, letting in the bright morning sun. Like the gown, I despised it. My father had emphasized knowledge and education as the true treasure. Our home had basic furnishings, with only a few simple decorations for use when entertaining company. I was unused to such riches and found the abundance of them revolting.

There was a table draped in linen and filled with food, presumably for breaking my fast. Dates, grapes, wines, loaves of bread, a wedge of cheese, smoked meats, and other food-laden platters covered the table. The combination of the food with the smell of the incense nauseated me. Crossing over to the brazier, I closed it. That took care of the incense. Glancing at the table, I realized I was a little hungry. I selected some fruits and topped them with honey and yogurt before eating daintily. I reclined on a chaise while eating, gazing outside at the garden.

Exhaustion swept through me, making my eyelids heavy. I'd never stayed up all night before. I'd had no idea how tired it would make me.

Dunyazade appeared, with dark circles under her bloodshot eyes. She looked as exhausted as I felt.

"I was hoping to study, but instead—" I began.

"Sleep." She sat the study materials on a table and instead arranged some cushions before drifting off in slumber.

I was mere moments behind her. Staying awake all night had drained me more than I thought it would.

After a rather lengthy nap, we finally turned our attention to the books and scrolls Dunyazade had brought with her. Despite my best intentions, however, I could not focus on knowledge. I kept reliving the previous night in my head.

"Sutai? Sutai!" Duny rolled her eyes when I finally acknowledged her. "I know you are overwhelmed, but surely you can at least focus on mathematics?"

I played with the sheaf of parchment in front of me. Not one calculation worked out. I sighed.

Duny's face fell. "I'm worried too."

"It's more than worry, Duny." I stood. "What if this doesn't work? What if he figures it out? Then what?" I should be glad of the additional time to live, the additional day for Dunyazade and my father to share together. Instead, jealousy took hold. I walked across the room, my feet scuffing the fluffy rug. I leaned out of the window, straining for a glimpse of my father's house. The wall surrounding the palace and the other nearby estates blocked my view. "I just want to go home."

Duny didn't say anything. I felt hot tears growing in my eyes.

"Well, last night was a success. Just—take it one day at a time." Duny crossed the room and draped an arm around me, giving me a squeeze. "Last long enough to find a way out of this. I'll help as much as I can."

"What would I do without you," I murmured. I closed my eyes and focused on the delicious warmth of the setting sun on my face. If only I could live in this moment, make this instant last a thousand days.

Someone clearing their throat distracted me from my reverie. As one, Duny and I turned toward the entrance.

One of the guards from earlier stood there, somewhat embarrassed. "The sultan has sent for you, Majesty. I would suggest you come quickly. He has been rather out of sorts today."

I arched a brow. "I guess a morning without spilling blood makes for a poor day?" Why should I care if the Sultan was having a bad day? He clearly didn't care about the torment he put me through.

The guard's face flushed. "I didn't say that, my lady—"

"You didn't need to." I straightened my veil, then whispered to Duny, "Don't go far—please. We will need to repeat last night."

To her credit, Dunyazade fought valiantly to hide the exhaustion I knew she felt. She merely nodded, then returned to the table to focus on learning. She would finish the studying I couldn't even begin.

I strode over to the guard and waited for him to escort me away.

The sultan was waiting in the prayer niche. Without a word, I retrieved my prayer rug and laid it out. I felt the sear of his gaze burning on me but maintained my composure—for now. His lip curled up in disgust. I squelched the rising feeling of satisfaction inside of me. It would not do to lose my control now. As one, we knelt on the rugs and began the evening prayers. Rather than be distracted, I devoted my entire being to the worship of Allah.

When the prayers concluded, I rolled up my rug and returned it to the holder, still maintaining absolute silence. The sultan watched me, eyes flickering across my features with consideration.

"I will take my evening meal now," he announced.

I gave him a crisp nod.

"After that, you will be ready to receive me in my chambers."

Again, I gave nothing more than a simple nod. My heart pounded against my ribs.

"You will finish the story." He whirled about and strode off.

I returned to my room, hands trembling in fear.

Duny looked up at me and noticed my expression. "We can do this. Together."

Chapter 3
Day 19: Shahryar

My vision dimmed. With a jerk, I shook myself awake. Several nights of almost no sleep was catching up to me.

That woman...*your wife*, the voice inside my head insisted. She had finished the first story by launching into another, spinning the tale into a twisted snarl of a plot that would take a good fortnight to untangle. I accepted her presence for the meantime. At least she was entertaining, which was more than any of the other sniveling brats had been.

Married for nineteen days. Every time I reflected on it, I felt as though I was standing in the midst of a swirling dust storm. It was never supposed to be like this. I was a ruler, a sultan—my word was law. And for the past eighteen days, I had broken my own law. Shame filled me. After the ultimate betrayals I had endured, I vowed to suffer no wife to live long enough to betray me thus again. Yet tradition, a convention stronger than the oldest and most respected laws, dictated that a ruler be a married man. My lips twisted into a snarl. Tradition or no, I would never be deceived again.

My attendant started at the expression on my face. I schooled myself to calmness again. It would not do to frighten my retinue. He tucked a final piece of robe before bowing and leaving the dressing chamber. I sighed. I would have to send word along, somehow, that he was not to blame for my mood.

Everyone at the palace seemed to walk on eggshells now. I knew my recent surliness came largely from insufficient sleep, with no small part of it directed to how my latest wife seemed to thrive on innocently bending my will.

She was already waiting for me in the hallway. Dressed impeccably, not a hair or stitch out of place, was my newfound aggravation: Sutaita. Her icy demeanor echoed the coldness of my veins. There was no love between us—in fact, I rather doubted that love, true love, existed. But that did not matter. Our marriage was not one of love.

For the past eighteen mornings, I had greeted her with the derision I felt for her entire gender. Liars and cheaters, all of them. Yet my insults and sneers rolled off of her like water on oil. Nothing broke her glacial expressions.

Perhaps it was time to try something different. If anger did nothing, mayhap kindness would be her downfall. I stopped short. Could I become like those I hated most? Could I fool her into thinking me changed into an amiable, content husband? Her eyes narrowed as she regarded me. No, I could not trick her. She was clever—too intelligent for her own good.

Nevertheless, I decided to try. "Good morning, dearest wife. How was your sleep?" Despite my best efforts, disdain flowed from my voice. I would never be able to hide my true feelings, not really.

A shadow crossed her face. It was so fleeting, I wondered if I had only imagined it. Before I could consider, she responded. "My rest was sufficient, my lord. And yours?"

Damn woman, always asking me questions. She was sneaky, waiting until I spoke first, as decorum demanded. I glared at her. "Fine." I stalked off toward the prayer niche.

She followed, head high, as though she was actually leading me and I just happened to be in front of her. I went through the motions of praying—I always went through the motions, as actual prayer brought me no peace anymore. Yet Sutaita—she always seemed completely absorbed in her devotions. I was supposed to be a representative of the Prophet, a leader of my people in every sense. When I compared my faith to hers, however, I found it lacking—another reason why I couldn't stand the sight of her. How embarrassing that I, a spiritual leader, had less faith than a woman?

As we concluded, I considered my decree. I could summon her with me, order her beheaded, and be done with the whole mess. But then I wouldn't know how it ended. The story had a caliph remarkably like Father in it, and the kalandars—

I realized that Sutaita was staring at me, waiting for instructions. "You're dismissed." I turned and stalked off. Surely, it could wait until tomorrow. Then I could hear the end of the story. And tonight, no matter how sweetly Dunyazade implored, no doubt part of the whole thing, I would refuse to hear another word. I would hear the end of this story, and that would be it. I could slay the upstart Sultana without regret.

Ja'far studied me as I entered the court. Various courtiers and sheikhs awaited to dance attendance on me, and a queue of supplicants awaited the commencement of official hearings for the day. Ja'far seemed to be searching for someone, and then relaxed when he noticed I was alone. Sutaita was his daughter—something I kept forgetting.

"Tomorrow," I snarled at him before taking my seat.

He nodded, wisely choosing not to speak. The hours went on, and I did my best to listen fairly and impartially to the supplicants. When it came time for the noon meal, however, I ended court proceedings. I was simply too distracted. Ja'far accompanied me to the gardens.

"Your Majesty—is there a reason you are only holding court for half a day?"

I grunted. "Too distracted."

"I see." Ja'far continued to tail me, much to my irritation. "I noticed that—"

"Your daughter is safe for another night," I interrupted. "Now leave me alone."

He halted. I continued striding down the hall. The sound of footsteps told me that he was dogging after me again.

"Your Majesty—I am your advisor. I cannot help you if you refuse to confide in me." Ja'far was relentless—a trait I used to admire in him. He was also loyal—and proved his loyalty beyond a doubt when he offered Sutaita as a bride.

My cheeks grew warm with embarrassment. I should at least give him the opportunity to perform his duties. "Sutaita is—different. I don't know what to make of her." I looked over to the Vizier.

Ja'far nodded.

"But what if she is the same? What if she would be just like the others?"

Ja'far considered for a moment. "I must admit that I am biased in this. However, I can attest to my daughter's character. She is devout, faithful, and considerate." He scratched his chin, pondering. "Have you tried talking to her? Getting to know her?"

I shrugged. "Why?"

"Was it only women who betrayed you?"

"They—"

"Was it only women?"

Silence bloomed between us. The cold ice of rage filled my veins as I remembered the events that led to my edict. I sighed, releasing the anger—for now. "No," I whispered. "My brother as well."

"Ah," he answered. "Your brother as well. Tell me, do you blame me for your brother's transgressions?"

I shook my head, the warmth of humiliation returning.

"Then why would you blame Sutaita for the faults of your first wife?"

I couldn't answer him. It was as though a stone had lodged itself in my throat, keeping me from even a sound of acknowledgment. To his credit, Ja'far bowed and left me, without censure or judgment, to the meal that tasted like dust in my mouth.

That night, while Sutaita took up her story again, I watched her. Really watched her. Gone was the cold reserve from the morning. Her lips parted and swished as she spoke, forming words with tones both dulcet and mysterious. And her eyes—I could lose myself in their rich, bistre depths. The familiar stirrings of attraction and care rose in my chest. I hadn't felt that in years. And the time I'd felt it, it had been false. A lie. Was this also a lie?

"One more story, Your Majesty?" Dunyazade's voice pierced through my reverie.

How could I refuse? Between the seduction of Sutaita's story and the child-like gregariousness of Dunyazade's request, I could not say no. Despite my best intentions, I nodded, and Sutaita began another saga.

Chapter 4
Day 93: Sutaita

After several months of marriage, I had the routine down. Wake, dress, and pray. Go to the lavish room that served as my prison. Nibble on breakfast until Dunyazade arrived. Spend the majority of the day in study and contemplation. Pray the midday prayers with the sultan. Bid Dunyazade farewell, then pray the evening prayers with the sultan. Eat a solitary dinner, then pray and prepare for bed. Say the final night prayers before welcoming Dunyazade again. Tell stories for a few hours. Fall asleep.

And the sultan—he still didn't know what to do about me. He avoided me as much as he could. Except for stories at night and prayers throughout the day, I never saw him. In fact, Dunyazade was the only companion I had. Loneliness gnawed at me, filling me. Although I'd never been much of a socialite, I now missed all the human contact I'd taken for granted, from fellow scholars to vendors at the market. Sure, there were servants and guards. But they kept to themselves, afraid to get close to me only to lose me to the inevitable.

And that was a whole new level of torture—one I hadn't planned on when concocting my scheme. Waking each morning in fear of losing my life was taking its toll on my health.

"Sometimes I wish he would just end this and kill me."

Duny looked up from the book she was studying, eyes wide in alarm. "Surely, you don't mean that."

I shrugged. "I still don't know what to do about him. He's always so angry. I thought, maybe—"

"Just keep trying. He can't stay mad at you forever—especially when you didn't do anything to him." While her tone was warm and comforting, her face still held the tension of earlier.

I smiled and shook my head. "Sister, you always think the best of people. What if he can't be happy? What if whatever happened to make him pass this edict never goes away?"

Dunyazade considered. "It is a problem. But you love problems."

"I worry that this time I've bitten off more than I can chew." I pursed my lips. Duny was right—I did know how to solve problems. In fact, I had chosen this partly to see if I could manage this particular conundrum. But how to begin?

Dunyazade put her book down and stretched. "I need to head home. Father will be ready for dinner soon." She studied me, as if unsure that she could leave without me doing harm to myself.

I nodded absently, still focused on the sultan and the problem he presented. "Of course. See you tonight." Hopefully she understood that she had successfully engaged my thoughts. Problem-solving always cured melancholia when that mood struck.

She smiled. "Until tonight, Sutaita." With a quick hug, she was on her way.

I spent another minute gazing out the window. I never thought I would miss the noise and bustle of town. A sharp rap behind me caught my attention.

One of my guards cleared his throat. "Your Majesty, your presence is requested in court."

I stared at him. I had not been to the throne room since my wedding night. The blood rushed out of my face. This was it. He had decided to execute me. And I hadn't even really said goodbye to Dunyazade. And Father—he would be forced to watch. My hands trembled.

"My lady, if you please?"

I swallowed. Somehow, I forced my feet to move. Everything around me slowed. My heart pounded. Try as I might to think of a solution, my mind was blank. We turned down the main corridor, murmurs of conversation echoed down the hall. My escort nodded, and the two guards manning the enormous double doors stepped aside. The doors opened, the soft whisper of conversation grew into a full-fledged babble. I looked down, following my escort meekly toward the throne.

The sultan sat there, Father slightly behind him to the right. A man and woman were in front of the throne, clearly supplicants regarding some law or provision. I looked up at my father, confused.

"There she is. I will have my wife hear your complaint and advise me." The sultan gestured to a small seat beside him. "Sit, and listen well."

I wasted no time obeying him.

"Now, tell us your story again."

The man fidgeted, shifting his weight from side to side. "It's like this: I work hard, growing food and tending the herds. This—woman—she lives well in my home. We have been married nearly a year. She refuses to allow me my husbandly rights. How am I to get a son? What should a man do with such a woman?"

At this, many of the sheikhs in attendance made noises of agreement. The sultan turned to smirk at me, enjoying what he thought would be a difficulty for me. By now, he probably felt confident assuming I had no sexual experience. We certainly hadn't engaged in such intimacy. And my father's reputation was such that the sultan could feel confident of my innocence in that regard.

He then held up his hand for silence. "Well, my wife? How do you advise?"

I met his eyes with mine. This was surely a test, a means to see what I would do in front of a large audience. To see if I could pass logical, fair, impartial judgment, without the emotional shortcomings many men assumed my gender possessed. And what did this man value most of all? His anger at my dogged persistence in keeping him hanging each night with a story was a clue He wanted appreciation, respect. He wanted power and control—except that he didn't actually want that; he only thought he did. If he actually wanted those things, I'd have been dead nearly a fortnight now.

So then what he truly wanted, in his heart of hearts, was the thing I'd just pined for moments before: companionship, trust, someone he could rely on, someone who would understand the difficult judgments he would pass and not lose respect or love for him while supporting him through it.

Ironically, that was a role I could fill perfectly. I preferred logical judgments free of emotional entanglements. My love of mathematics was born from my adoration of pure, simple, reason. I could never care for someone less because they had to pass a fair, just sentence on someone. The thought terrified me in both its permanence and plausibility.

But first, his pride. He didn't know he wanted this. So respect, appreciation, and decorum before all else. "Your Majesty, first let me thank you for your trust in me. I am honored at the opportunity to advise you and celebrate your willingness to hear my counsel."

He snorted.

I wasn't surprised. He probably didn't believe me. So trust, then, was the biggest issue.

I turned to the couple and addressed the husband first. "When you married your bride, what were you contractually obligated to do based on your nikah?"

The man's face turned ashen. He mumbled something under his breath.

"You will answer Her Majesty," my guard said.

The man lifted his chin. "To house her, feed her, and clothe her."

"And have you fulfilled that agreement?"

The man's face paled again, and he shook his head.

"I see." I focused on the woman. "What is he doing to work toward providing for you?"

The woman met my eyes. "Nothing. He drags me here, complaining of me—while he spends all the money I try to save for our household on drink and gambling. Such a man is not a husband to any woman."

"Can you prove this allegation?" the sultan asked, leaning forward.

The woman bowed her head but answered, "Ask his friends. You will hear the truth."

The sultan gestured to some guards across the throne room, who saluted and marched out. "We will hear soon enough."

"While we wait, I would advise you both, if you would hear it," I murmured.

The sultan rolled his eyes, but the woman nodded. Her husband merely shrugged.

Now was my chance. I had to show respect, true, but show compassion and love as well. Show that in me was safety. I pushed down the butterflies in my stomach, ignoring the goosebumps swelling on my arms. "Remember how the Q'uran tells us marriage should be—like clothing. You should be as close to each other as clothing is to bare skin. Not just physically," I admonished the husband, "but emotionally. How can you be close to your wife when you are not at home?"

I shifted my gaze to the wife. "And if you are close with him physically, mayhap he will seek out your company instead of the gambling dens."

I stood. "Our clothing protects us from heat, sand, and storm. You should seek to protect your wife. What if you perish tomorrow? With no savings, no financial security, how will she live? Why would she want to share your bed when you have failed to provide even the most basic means for her? She claims that she tries to save, to help prosper your house. Mayhap she would be amenable to a child if she knew there was the ability to care for one."

I swallowed. My throat was dry, but I pushed on. "Clothing makes us beautiful; we decorate our bodies with it. You should seek to decorate each other, praise each other, find faith and devotion in each other. Do you pray together? Mayhap you should start."

The sultan shifted at this. I turned to face him, dropping the emotional guards I'd built around myself to survive his constant emotional onslaught. "I pray all of the five prayers with my husband. No matter what happens in our day, we take those moments to unite together in praise for Allah. In this, he has decorated me beyond compare."

The sultan's face reddened, but whether in embarrassment or anger, I could not tell. Something in his eyes caught mine. For the first time, I saw an emotion that was not rage or anger. Was it shame?

My words caught in my throat. Why did I do that? Why did I reveal anything about myself to this monster of a man? In that split second, I'd given him power over me. *Please, don't let him hurt me for one second of ineptitude.*

I turned away from his intense gaze and refocused on the couple. "And our clothing should be comfortable, something we can be relaxed in, something that gives us freedom and security at the same time. Why do you seek to bring your private quarrel to the public eye? Both of you? Surely, you could have addressed this yourself by having an honest conversation? If not alone, reached out to a married couple whom you admire, and asked their advice? Both of you are shamed in our eyes."

The breathless guards returned. The sultan raised his eyebrows, questioning. They nodded. He rose. I stepped back into a curtsy.

"My wife speaks with wisdom beyond her time. Leave us. Resolve this, or request a divorce. But do not sully my court with bickering."

The man and his wife left. Guards began ushering people out of the palace. The court was adjourned. I began my return to my chambers for the evening meal.

"Sutaita—wait."

I halted. I must obey him.

"How did you know what to say to that couple? No woman knows her religion that well." I turned to face him. For the first time, a genuine look of question was on his face, instead of derision or contempt.

"I am a hadith scholar. I have made it a habit to review religious text and read from the Q'uran regularly. Allah knows all—any problem we have, we simply need to bring it before Him, and the truth will be made known to us. I am merely a vessel for His knowledge." I curtsied, murmuring, "My lord."

That night, as I took up the story again, he sat silent and still, staring at me. After a few hours, he rose. "Dunyazade, I must ask you to visit again on the morrow. It is late, and the Sultana and I both need sleep."

Dunyazade rose and curtsied before slipping out of the chamber.

I tried to swallow the lump in my throat. Would he strike now, with no witnesses? Having failed to kill me immediately, did he seek another, easier solution?

The sultan studied me with dark, glittering eyes. "Sutaita, your endurance is remarkable. But I must have more than a few hours' sleep tonight. Would you be accepting of a shorter evening storytime?"

The question took me completely off guard. He was asking *me* permission? What had happened in that throne room? How had one fleeting glance completely changed him from the surly, demanding man he'd been the past few weeks?

I tried my best to smile, although I imagine I only managed to look queasy. "Of course, my lord. As you wish."

He caught my chin in his hand, drawing me close. "As close as clothing, you said. Emotionally. I will try to work on this, Sutaita."

I felt as if I'd forgotten how to breathe. His eyes, when not hardened in hate, were a lovely, soft brown, luxurious and rich. The warmth of his hand on my chin, strong but not forceful, sent a shiver down my spine. Why was my body reacting this way? What was happening?

As I returned his gaze, I saw something I didn't understand. Something that thrilled and terrified me. And something new bloomed in my chest: hope.

Chapter 5
Day 129: Sutaita

That morning, at the conclusion of prayers, instead of silently escorting me to my chamber, the sultan invited me to break the fast with him in the garden.

"My lord?" I was so astonished, my usual composure evaporated.

He sighed. "I told you I would try, Sutaita. Try to be closer. Emotionally. This is a start, yes?" His eyes, normally hard as black diamonds, appeared soft and earnest, as they had when we'd first looked at each other openly. He actually meant to set aside time to spend with me.

My heart fluttered, that stirring of hope flittering through me again. Not trusting myself to speak, I nodded.

He smiled and held out a hand, offering to escort me. "I told the servants to prepare our breakfast in the garden," he confided.

How changed he was. No sneers, no derision. Could I trust it? Or was this another test, another trap. I thought back on that day in court as we walked to the gardens. Clearly, I'd done something right, teased out the correct response using inductive reasoning. And just as surely, he knew of the parable of marriage being as clothes. It was not exactly an exceptional or rare teaching; most couples were counseled on it before marriage. And although the parable was not recited at our wedding, he would expect me to be familiar with basic tenets of Islamic marriage, wouldn't he?

So then it wasn't what I said, but maybe that I chose to say it? A sliver of guilt stabbed at me. I'd exaggerated my regard for the sultan. Did he think that, after his short and dismissive treatment, I felt regard for him? How could I tell him that I'd read the situation and decided he needed someone to partner with, not someone to make his life harder, and that my speech was just that: my way of showing support.

The sound of rushing water tore me from my thoughts. The gardens of the palace in Baghdad were amazing. Green abounded, and the rush of water coursing throughout echoed off the palace walls. The scent of dates and orchids filled the air. In the middle of all this splendor, a well-laden table awaited. I silently began serving the food, first to a plate for my

31

husband. His eyebrows rose at this unexpected courtesy from me. Inside, I smiled to myself. In his frustration over me, he had forgotten that I was the daughter of his chief vizier and no stranger to courtly behavior and conduct. Once he took his seat, I followed suit, waiting again for him to begin eating before sampling the food myself. If this was, indeed, a test, I knew then that I had passed.

His eyes stayed on me, a curious look on his face. Several moments elapsed in silence.

Had I done something wrong? Mayhap I hadn't passed the test, whatever it was, after all. He was waiting for me to make a gaff, to expose myself as a woman, and therefore weak and prone to fault. With years' of patience gained through meditating and studying, I simply waited.

Finally, he broke the silence. "Sutaita, you puzzle me."

I gazed at him but held my silence. It was, after all, my best option.

He seemed to expect more. He waited a second longer, then continued, "I had sworn to never trust, never have faith, never suffer any woman ever again. And yet here you are, months later. Your behavior is most circumspect. You conduct yourself with perfect modesty and grace. And your stories..." His eyes shifted, gaining a faraway look of wonder.

"If I may, my lord, ask you a question?" I held my breath. He must not know the paralytic fear coursing through me. My heart hammered as I fought to maintain my calm demeanor.

His eyes became sharp, questioning, distrustful. "Of course." He leaned back, his eyes narrowing even more.

I feared that I had overstepped my bounds. I could not ask what I wanted to ask—which was why he hated women so. While that question was at the tip of my tongue, I knew I could not ask it—not yet.

Instead, I gave him a bow of my head and asked the sultan, "In many of my stories are jinn who grant wishes. If you were to find one such jinni, what would you wish for?" While not the question that weighed on me, it was a diversion. Ironic that my life now consisted of diverting this man from sending for the headsman.

The sultan's eyes widened in surprise; then his brow furrowed in thoughtfulness. "Hmm. You know, I never think about things like that." His hand rose to his mouth, one finger tapping on his cheek.

He was so altered in that moment from the angry and derisive man I had previously seen that I nearly laughed. He looked like a pupil thinking at his studies. Despite my efforts to remain emotionless, my lips drew back in a small grin.

He smiled at me, his deep brown eyes twinkling. "I would wish for the wisdom of Solomon, that I could control many jinn. That I, too, could have such a lasting legacy."

His enthusiasm thoroughly disarmed me. "A remarkable wish. But surely you have established your legacy?"

His mood dampened. "I feel...stuck. I have reunified the empire and strengthened the might of this nation, but I feel that there must be...more." He looked out over the garden. "Sometimes, I wonder what might have been if I had acted differently." He shrugged and began eating.

His answer, rather than provide any illumination, only puzzled me more. When he spoke of the Empire, there was passion and love in his voice and eyes. A yearning had filled his countenance when he spoke of legacy. His father, the previous sultan, had certainly left large shoes to fill. And yet, despite this desire, this burning need to meet and surpass the legacy laid upon him, he'd chosen one of death and pain. Curiosity surged through me. Did he regret his murderous ways? Wish he had chosen differently during the civil fighting?

"What more do you imagine doing?" There, I asked. He could answer or dismiss me—whichever pleased him.

He hesitated before answering, "My father accomplished so much. Building the House of Wisdom, leading this Empire in scientific and mathematical discovery—it all makes me feel so inadequate, as though I should be doing something more, something greater, exceeding his legacy."

"I know what you mean. When I was younger, I had such ambitions..." I bit my lip. *Too forward!* I warned myself. But to my amazement, the sultan did not seem upset. He looked curious.

"You know, we have been married now for over a hundred days, and yet I know nothing about you. Nothing except that you tell the most fascinating and enrapturing stories."

"I might point out that I know nothing of you, my lord, except that you keep postponing my death—"

His face immediately hardened, the old, familiar anger returning to his eyes.

"—for which I am most grateful. I do owe you, for today at least, my life."

Something crossed his countenance, too quick and turbulent for me to recognize or understand. How could one man be so difficult to pin down? And had I gained valuable information at the cost of this seeming truce between us? My heart thumped so hard, I'm surprised he didn't hear it over the cascading waterfall next to us.

"Thank you for dining with me. Please await me in your chamber."

I rose, bowing in obedience and turning to leave. The lump in my throat refused to leave.

"Until tonight, Sutaita."

Relief rushed through me. I had, for the moment, at least one more night.

That night, he met me in my room earlier than usual. Dunyazade was attending me, as was her habit. The table was covered in opened books, and I was working out a mathematical error. When he entered, we both rose hurriedly to drop into respectful curtsies.

"Sutaita—and Dunyazade. Good evening. I wanted to partake of the evening meal with you. If you are willing, that is."

Dunyazade frowned. She normally ate dinner at home with Father, then returned to listen to the rest of a story. Luckily for both of us, storytime had diminished to be only an hour or two long, instead of an all-night affair. She also knew that I was left to my own devices whenever she wasn't here. Her eyes flicked back and forth between the sultan and me.

For my part, I was so stunned that it took me a moment to find words to respond. "Your Majesty, I would be honored. But my sister—"

"She is invited as well. And I can send for your father. We— Let's make it a family dinner."

Dunyazade smiled. "How kind of you. Thank you for the invitation." She looked over her shoulder at me, panic flashing across her face as she excused herself, presumably to wash for the meal.

I could only hope my face did not mirror hers. A family dinner. Did it mean he'd changed his mind? Surely even he would not torment my father by partaking of a meal only to slaughter me the next day. I turned it over and over in my head but could not make sense of it.

I stepped forward to look up into his eyes. "To what do we owe the esteem, my lord?"

His eyes met mine. "It is my wish to honor my wife—and her family."

My cheeks warmed slightly. It was the first time he had ever treated me with respect, let alone honor.

Chapter 6
Day 193: Shahryar

I had come to enjoy my mornings with Sutaita. She usually didn't say much, instead choosing her words carefully and voicing them when they would have the most impact. She also appeared to love the gardens, and the adornment of her sculpted yet soft face completed my view. *Stop that*, I told myself.

"Lovely morning," I said, relishing the splash of water and the scent of green. I sought Sutaita's gaze.

Eyes downcast, a shadow covered her face. It was Sutaita—genuinely Sutaita—without the mask she constantly wore around me. I held in a sigh. She was not happy here.

How could she be happy? Every day she wakes up waiting for you to kill her. The thought nearly made me wince. It was akin to how prisoners were tortured. But the alternative...could I trust her?

As it did every time I asked myself this question, my mind turned to that fateful day in court. She'd looked at me, earnest and faithful, naught but complete and open honesty as she confessed how praying together decorated her beyond compare. It was then when I realized how beautiful she looked, especially when we prayed. It surpassed even the engaging and magnetic deportment she had when storytelling.

But apart from those times, sorrow. Always sorrow filled those bistre eyes, and in my heart of hearts, I knew I was the cause of the sadness filling her entire being.

But what could I do? I didn't dare change anything now and look weak. Maybe I could change, could face my sheikhs with that alteration, if I knew I could trust her. And the circle repeated itself.

Ja'far's advice echoed in my ears. At this point, what did I have to lose?

I cleared my throat. "Sutaita?"

She looked up, darkness fleeing from her features. The mask was back on, and the shield she wore struck at my very core. I hated seeing her but not really seeing her.

"I was thinking—you tell me stories every night. I—" I hesitated. Once I did this, there would be no turning back. "I think I should like to tell you a story. If you would hear it."

The ghost of a smile crossed her features. "As it pleases you, my lord."

Panic seized me, stilling my throat. Now, what story should I tell? I recalled the ever-present, ever hidden sadness. Sadness I understood. Sadness was something we could share.

"When I was barely more than a youth, my father became very ill..."

I was waiting with my brother. We were both outside the royal chambers. I was pacing, too anxious to stand still. Attendants and guards flocked around us. The women had been dismissed after their tears and wailing grated on one too many nerves. Father was inside his room, abed, attended only by a medic.

The doors to the chamber opened. The medic summoned Muhammad and me. Courtiers rose to follow, but the medic shook his head. "Only the Chief Vizier may attend."

The Chief Vizier, Tahmores, smiled smugly as he edged ahead of the other courtiers to join Muhammad and me.

The medic whispered to us once we entered the large room, "He is near the end. Please try to avoid causing him any distress."

I nodded at the medic's words.

All three of us approached the bed. Father's skin was tinged gray, his eyes half-lidded, as if opening them fully was too exhausting. He seemed to struggle slightly for each breath. It broke my heart. I admired this man so much. He could easily have dismissed me, the son of a mere concubine. Instead, he showered me with love, attention, and honor—as much as he was able to bestow. My heart squeezed with sorrow.

"My...sons...my time grows short," he rasped.

Muhammad stood solid, firm in demeanor. I wondered if he was in denial. It was likely he would be sultan 'ere evening passed. How would I feel in his position? Afraid, surely—what a legacy to live up to, that of Harun al-Rashid. The responsibility of merely maintaining the vast Empire, with its stores of knowledge and wonder, was incredible.

Yet Muhammad seemed eager. Maybe, since he had trained and studied for this, he felt ready, excited to prove himself, to take charge and demonstrate the leadership he felt he possessed. I wondered, and not for the first time, if studying to become the sultan had poisoned Muhammad's relationship with Father, if instead of a parent, he saw only a rival claimant or an unnecessary chaperon.

"I have decided...I must...not follow my edict...at the cost of the kingdom..."

Everyone in the room started. What could that mean? My heart began hammering against my ribs. Had he lost his mind? This should not have even been a question—it had been decided years ago.

"Allah will be displeased if I favor a younger son...over...an older one...so..." A coughing fit overtook him.

I glanced sidelong at my brother. Muhammad's features seemed unaltered, but something burned in his eyes. I shuddered despite myself.

"The empire...will be...given...to Shahryar."

The sound of a gasp reached me, and it was a moment before I realized it was my own. Muhammad's lips tightened. Tahmores only looked perplexed. I opened and closed my mouth several times, feeling like a fish. What could I possibly say? *No thank you, Father, I have no desire to inherit your legacy?* And Muhammad. What a blow to him.

It was Tahmores who finally broke the silence. "Your Majesty, I know we spoke of this in the past, but I thought the matter settled. Surely, Allah would prefer that the sultan be a royal representative and not the get of a whore?"

I hung my head, ashamed. I was never able to escape my mother's identity. Never mind that she had been selected to be in the sultan's harem, chosen to be a concubine, a companion. That honor began and ended at the bordello. Muhammad turned and began to stalk out before thinking the better of it and halting just in front of the doors.

I lifted my head, my eyes meeting my father's. "Please, Father..." Even I wasn't certain what I was begging for—was it an easy solution to this quandary? Was it for him to stand resolute? I couldn't even begin to decide how I felt, for I had never thought to reach so highly for myself.

"I...love you...my son..." And with that, my father died.

The medic rushed in, poking and prodding. I clutched my father's hand, a whirlwind of emotions rushing through me: the surprise of Father's proclamation; the empathy and understanding for Muhammad, who surely felt betrayed; and as I clutched the limp, lifeless hand in mine, the overwhelming sorrow of loss. *I'm not ready for this. I'm not ready to live life without a father.* I fought back tears but to no avail. They surged past my eyelids, reminding me as this entire situation did of the frighteningly small amount of control any of us had over life and death.

It seemed like hours before the medic turned, sorrow shadowing his eyes. "The sultan is dead. May he find peace with Allah." He bowed and quietly quit the room.

A slamming sound startled me. Muhammad had punched the wall. I looked at him, astonished. How could he behave so at such a time?

Tahmores remained calm. "Your Highness, your father is barely cooled. Surely, we can resolve any, um, differences of opinion, at a later date?"

Muhammad looked up, his eyes wild with anger. I glanced back at Father. I could not handle Muhammad and his misplaced rage. Surely, he knew that I would never rob him—he was my brother! And now the only family I had left in all the world. I should say something, do something, but I couldn't. Muhammad must simply be upset because he didn't know what I would do. I needed to talk to him, reassure him, let him know that his love and brotherhood meant more to me than a crown.

I don't know what further passed between the gaze of Tahmores and Muhammad, but Muhammad eventually stalked out of the room.

Tahmores approached me. "I am sorry, Shahryar. I wish you were allowed time to mourn, but we must act fast if we are to secure your inheritance."

I whirled around. "I don't want an inheritance. I want my father back." I turned back to the bed. "I don't want to fight with Muhammad. He is my only family." Bile rose in my throat. How could anyone only think of politics now? My father was dead. My brother presumed I would betray him. There was no one I could turn to, no one I could trust.

Tahmores sighed. "Shahryar, I know. But your father was right to make this decision."

I snorted. "A whore's get? You said yourself that you did not wish this."

I studied the vizier's face. It was lined, and gray hairs framed his sagging cheeks. Underneath wispy white brows, his eyes were soft, an expression I was not accustomed to seeing on his face. Tahmores sighed. "I just wish he had spoken it sooner. Muhammad is not fit for rule. He is too...harsh. Too rash. Please, son—"

That was one insult too many. "I am not your son," I whispered. I stood up, determined to soldier on. I needed to mend fences with my brother, and quickly. For the good of the empire, I needed him to know that I didn't want the throne, didn't want any of it—I only desired his brotherly love and affection. It was my only hope, my only chance, at saving my family. I strode out of the bedchamber.

As soon as I exited, a pair of guards grabbed my wrists and clapped me in irons. I stopped, astonished. I searched the room. Most of the courtiers had left, but the few who remained sneered at me.

And at the opposite end of the room stood my brother, a malevolent smile curled across his face. "Put the murderer in the dungeon." He whirled on his heel and left.

The guards hustled me down a different hall. My mind was reeling. A murderer? What was going on? Why was Muhammad acting this way? "Please—I need to speak to my brother."

The guards just forced me along, ignoring me. I continued asking the entire descent into the dungeon, begging even as they threw me in a cell and bolted the door. I clutched at the bars in the window, calling after them. They never even turned back to acknowledge me.

What just happened? Muhammad knew I wasn't a murderer. What sort of prank was this? I rubbed my arms and began to pace, seeking to ward off a chill not brought on by the dank underground cell.

The overwhelming grief hit me. I was alone. Utterly and completely alone. No father, no brother, and no friends. If they believed the slanderous lie that I would kill an old man on his deathbed, they were no friends of mine. I sank to the floor and wept.

Hours later, I heard the door to the dungeon open and close. Tahmores walked down the corridor, glancing in the cells as he passed. He stopped outside of mine.

"Shahryar. There you are." His shoulders sagged. "What a mess."

I leaped to my feet. "What happened? Why am I locked up? I need to speak to Muh—"

Tahmores raised a hand, silencing me. "You cannot speak with your brother. Not yet." Sadness edged his eyes. "Muhammad left your father's room and immediately declared that you murdered him. I have been spending the better part of the day correcting the general knowledge of what transpired. Your brother will not be happy when he finds out, and my life will most likely be forfeit."

The reality of what Tahmores said hit me like a punch to the stomach. *How could Muhammad? Why didn't he just talk to me?*

Tahmores must have read my thoughts. "Your brother's actions are precisely why your father bestowed the inheritance upon you instead. Muhammad thinks only of himself and wants everything. You must stop thinking of him as a brother."

I turned away. This was too much to handle all at once. I loved Muhammad. We'd been inseparable growing up: sneaking treats from the kitchens, exploring the hills outside the city, even playing pranks in the palace. How could I just shut the door on all that history, all those feelings? Tahmores seemed to sense my grief. He withdrew, leaving me in silent and painful contemplation.

I remained in my cell for over a week. Tahmores came each day to visit me and notify me of the goings-on. Every time I saw him, or any other person, I pleaded that I might speak with Muhammad, assure him that his throne was safe—I had no intention of taking it. Muhammad never came.

When I was finally released, it was late at night with Tahmores and a guard. Apparently, Tahmores had bribed the guard and the palace staff to drug and evict my brother. The internal coup left me troubled. I wanted to mend fences with my brother, not sabotage what little trust remained between us.

I grabbed Tahmores' robes. "Please. Take me to him."

Tahmores took my hands and removed them from his clothing. "Highness—that is, Majesty, no."

"But I—"

"No. I told you, I am bound not to you, but to your father's dying wish. I have worked hard and sacrificed much to get even this opportunity. I will not see you squander it."

I attempted to nod, but inside, my blood boiled. If I was to be the ruler, how dare he order me around in that fashion? And if I did not want to be a ruler, he could not force me. I was older than my brother but still young, merely twenty-three years old. I knew I wasn't ready for this.

My escort took me to the baths, then to a secluded wing of the palace. No sense in putting me within easy reach of assassins, I presumed. I tried to sleep the rest of the night but couldn't. I still felt the anguish of my brother's betrayal. *And I'm not much better, even if I didn't authorize the action against him.*

The next morning, Tahmores appeared again. I wondered if the man ever slept. He smiled, then sat down and began to outline the plan for me. "While you were locked up, I worked tirelessly on your behalf. About half the aristocracy backs you. I have been able to reveal the truth, counter the traitor's lies."

I flinched when he called my brother a traitor.

Tahmores eyes narrowed on me. "He is a traitor. Your father made his wishes clear, even if he handled it rather poorly and at the last minute. Every action against you, the rightful sultan, is treason. Understand?"

I nodded. No sense in arguing with Tahmores. Inside, however, I clung to the hope of reconciliation. After how close we were, surely, Muhammad would see reason.

Tahmores relaxed and leaned back. "Good. As I said, about half the aristocracy backs you. The spy I left to watch your brother reports that he is retreating to the family seat to the west. He will probably attempt to gather an army to take the city by force. We should marshal our forces as well, perhaps request assistance from outside allies."

"Do as you see best, Tahmores. I..." Tears threatened to overtake me. It was all so fast. I felt like my father had just died moments ago, and I still needed to grieve. "I am not quite ready for all this."

Tahmores studied me. After a long moment, he nodded. "Very well. I do need you to appoint advisors and other positions. Some places are vacant because your father's appointees have sided with Muhammad."

"Appoint whomever you see fit." I stared at the ground. I couldn't make myself care.

"Majesty, if I were any lesser of a man, I would do as you just commanded and fill the positions with men loyal to me instead of you—and take over myself. Luckily for you, I am not. *Please*, you must start acting as a ruler."

I just shrugged. Tahmores pursed his lips, then announced that he would give me a day to acclimate before pushing me again. He departed, and I hoped I hadn't just lost my only true ally.

I felt as if I'd fallen into a deep pit, so deep that no sliver of sunlight reached it, and couldn't get out. My father. Our relationship had been...different. When he had been teaching me, when I first expected to inherit, those were my favorite times. When Muhammad's mother had insisted that her son be considered for the throne, the demeanor in my father changed. It had hurt, but that I understood. He couldn't be seen to show preference for a bastard son. Despite the common practice of naming the firstborn son, no matter the mother, as heir, it was different for a royal dynasty. Or, at least, that's what I was told. And since naming Muhammad was a break from that tradition, Father needed to tread carefully, to make it clear which son he favored.

That was why all of this felt so completely surreal. I had given up hope for the throne, relinquished that responsibility, years ago. And while Tahmores' seemed more annoyed than surprised by the change, Muhammad was genuinely caught off-guard, as was I.

My thoughts dwelled on Muhammad for the entire day. I couldn't even imagine how he felt.

The next day, I rose with the sun. After saying my morning prayers, I stared out into the dawn. He was out there, somewhere. Hiding. Scared. All because of me.

The sound of a throat clearing behind me drew my attention. I turned to see Tahmores standing there.

"Majesty. I trust you are feeling better today?"

I nodded. I had to turn away, for I still could not meet his eyes. "My brother...is he truly...?" My throat closed, and I could no longer speak.

"Yes, Sire. His greed and hunger for power have consumed him. If not for me, you would be dead."

Dead? No, I couldn't believe it. Muhammad wouldn't have killed me. Would he?

I whirled around and stared into Tahmores' eyes. I knew I must look half crazy, but I needed answers. "Show me proof."

Wordlessly, Tahmores opened his ever-present folder of important papers, riffled through the papers, and pulled one out. He extended his arm, showing the inked lettering so I could read it. The document was a writ of execution and had my brother's signature.

I swallowed, trying to smooth away the lump in my throat. So it was true. Inside, I screamed to deny it, to declare the document a forgery. But the part of me that stood apart from emotion recognized the writ for what it was. Tahmores was right.

"Why? Why did you change your mind?" I needed to know why Tahmores supported me, needed to know where his loyalty came from.

He met my gaze levelly and shrugged. "You are—well, were, prior to this bout of madness—the stronger leader. The empire has grown and needs the strongest leader possible. My devotion is to the empire first and foremost. Personal concerns must be...disregarded...in that light." His gaze drove into mine. "Make a note of that, Sultan."

I bit off an angry retort, nodding.

After studying me for a few more seconds, he gave a curt nod. "Good. Now prepare yourself. First, you address the attending sheikhs, and convince them of your readiness to rule."

I blinked the memories from my vision. Sutaita studied me with narrowed, analytical eyes.

"Say something, Sutaita."

She drew in a breath, then let it out. Her lips moved, but no words came forth. After a moment, she met my eyes. "Thank you for trusting me with this story, my lord. I—" She bit her lip. "I must confess to some confusion. Why is there no record of this in the House of Wisdom?" She frowned. "I studied the conflict, and it mentions nothing of you being imprisoned."

I shifted from side to side. "I suppressed the knowledge. It is embarrassing enough that the entire court knows I languished for over a week in prison. No need to ensure that all following generations know of my shame as well."

Sutaita's lips narrowed. She looked away. Her judgment angered me. I opened up, gave her the "more" she asked for, and this was how she repaid me?

I fumed. "Do you think me weak? That I valued family more than the realm? Or do you question my judgment regarding the history?" I rose and stomped over to her.

Eyebrows raised, she shook her head. "No, my lord. Never." I was so close, I could sense the trembling she hid under the veneer of confidence and logic.

"Good," I whispered before leaving the garden.

Stalking through the palace, I mulled the conversation over. Where had I gone wrong? She spoke of marriage, of closeness, but as soon as I began speaking of my past, she rejected me. It made me so furious. If this was how she reacted, why bother? What was the point of getting close to anyone who would betray me just like Muhammad? Just like *her*.

I stopped and rolled my shoulders, trying to ease the tension as I came to a decision. Sutaita was no better than any of the others, than any other person who would inevitably betray me.

I vowed to kill her as soon as she finished her current story.

One Thousand and One Days

Chapter 7
Day 214: Sutaita

Three weeks later, Shahryar was still trying, or so it seemed. We continued to take breakfast together in the garden. We spoke little, usually just enjoying the ambiance of water singing over stone and the bouquet or floral scents. I could sense that he still didn't trust me, but it appeared he was, in his own way, attempting to spend time with me and be close. I had related the change to Dunyazade; it amazed her as well.

In the back of my mind, however, one worry kept niggling at me.

What would happen when I ran out of stories? I still had plenty to tell, but I was not really any closer to a change in the edict. While Shahryar tried, that persistent mistrust—not meeting my eyes, avoiding anything overly personal—still grated at me.

I voiced my concern to Duny one afternoon.

She patted me on the back. "You're worried about nothing, Sutai. If he wanted to harm you, he'd have done it by now. It's been seven whole months."

I shrugged but held my tongue. "He told me about his father's death."

Dunyazade started. "He did what? But those records are sealed—not even the scholars who manage the House of Wisdom can access them!"

"But for some reason, he still told me." I turned and began pacing. "I just don't know what he meant by it. He said he would try—" I stopped, not wanting to share that moment, that intimate treasure, even with Dunyazade. It was the only glimmer of hope I'd had in many months. Since things hadn't changed that much, I hesitated to voice it, in case it was an ephemeral moment doomed to wisp away like fog under the harsh morning sun.

"Try what?" she asked.

I pressed my lips. "Try to be kinder, I think. I don't know anymore." There. Enough to satisfy Duny without going into the details of that day in court or the promise the sultan had made me.

Dunyazade returned to the table and began organizing the study materials. "It's past time for me to leave. Besides, tomorrow I must visit the

House. I need to return some things." She straightened up, gazing at me with wide eyes. "You'll be all right without me?"

With a conscious effort, I smoothed my face. "Of course. Enjoy the trip."

"Do you need anything checked out?" Duny slid the books into a satchel, followed by a few scrolls.

I shook my head. "No, I'll survive. But you will return the following day?"

Satchel packed, she walked over and took both of my hands in hers. "Inshallah, Allah willing, I promise, dear sister."

With a quick kiss on the cheek, she departed.

I glanced back out the window. The sun still shone well above the horizon. It was early in the afternoon, and the sultan would be at court for at least another two hours. My mind drifted back to the conversation we had shared. His father died, he was jailed, then released, while his traitor brother left court? I frowned. Something didn't add up. I could ask my father, but I doubted he would answer. While he had indulged most of our scholarly pursuits, politics was exclusively a man's business.

Another puzzle, then.

I looked around the room. Duny had taken most of the studying materials, so further intellectual work was out of the question. But what could I do for another two hours?

With a huff of annoyance, I stalked to the door. Two guards stood at attendance.

"Are there any other places in the palace I may visit?"

My question startled them. They glanced at each other, then back at me.

I crossed my arms and stared them down.

The guard to my right cleared his throat. "There is the family wing, of course, which houses the sultan's sleeping quarters, the bathing chambers, and the prayer room."

"What about a library? Or records room? Surely, important information like family births and marriages are tracked and kept somewhere?"

The guard on my left looked down.

The guard on the right maintained eye contact but shifted from side to side. "There is a small library. But usually women prefer to stroll in the garden or take tea or coffee—"

"Please take me to the library." I raised my chin.

The guard on the left looked positively green.

The guard on the right sighed, his shoulders drooping as if carrying a heavy yoke. "Follow me, Your Majesty."

I followed the guards toward the garden, but instead of entering, we swung around to the right. This hall was wider than most of the others in the palace and was lined with portraits. Slowing, I studied each image, my eyes drifting down from the top.

A man wearing soft lilac pantaloons with a darker blue overcoat approached. "These are the royal portraits, Your Majesty. Is there one in particular you wish to see?"

Still ambling down the hall, I considered. "The sultan's father—where is his portrait?"

"Follow me." The man led me and the guards further down the hall. I continued scanning over the portraits, despite my increased pace. Like all other corridors, this hall was gilded with gold and well lit. Beautiful hand-woven rugs lined the hall, opulent red and golden thread entwined in intricate patterns.

"Here you are, Your Majesty." The man bowed and left.

I focused my attention on the indicated portrait. I had never seen Sultan Harun al-Rashid, so I couldn't tell if the artist copied the strong eyes and determined jaw of the man or simply added them for aesthetic effect. The face reminded me of my husband's, but without the ever-present derision and anger. *But he hasn't been quite so irritable these past few days*, I scolded myself. Only two portraits hung past this one on the walls—the sultan's and his brother's, I presumed. His brother's portrait showed close-set eyes framed with lines that spoke of anger and resentment. I could see how someone could look at that portrait and think him proud or determined. But they had not seen Shahryar's brows knit together in anger to recognize the familial similarity for what it was. *What happened to him?* The question goaded me on.

One of the guards cleared his throat. "If you're finished exploring, should we escort you back to your chambers?"

Ignoring him, I continued down to the end of the hall. To my right was a large library with rows of shelves filled with books, scrolls, and loose sheaves of paper. As I entered, the scratching of pen on paper sounded on either side. A quick glance showed me scribes standing or sitting around the perimeter, taking notes.

I couldn't keep the smile from my face. The sounds, the smells of parchment and ink, the very feel of a room where study and learning took place—an ache bloomed in my chest. How I'd missed the House of Wisdom, missed even our family's frequent visits to booksellers.

As I entered the room, a harried-looking man rushed up and gave me the briefest bow. "Your Majesty. Can I help you?" His tone, clipped and brusque, intimidated me slightly.

I squared myself. This was no time to lose my nerve. "I wish to explore the records."

He rubbed his already unruly black hair, brows coming together. "I don't think that's possible, Your Majesty. These records are private and not for common citizens—"

"Excuse me, I did not catch your name."

"Eh—"

"Of course, if given access to the private records of my family, I would have no need of your name." I maintained a calm exterior to belie the inner thrill I felt. *Please don't call my bluff.* I could only imagine how the sultan might react to this.

This clerk was not the first man I'd needed to outwit to find information, however. While the House of Wisdom did permit female scholars, many men felt the need to enforce their authority via access to information. Everyone had a weakness: I presumed this man's was his need to remain employed. And for that, he would do well to remain outside the sultan's notice.

"Sir, you have a simple choice: allow me access, and no one except me and these guards need know you allowed me in, or deny me access, and I can inform my husband. You can gamble as to whether or not he is happy with your decision."

The clerk paled and stepped aside. "Of course, Your Majesty."

I smiled, and a surge of adrenaline coursed through me. *Victory.*

The records consisted of loose sheets bound into a simple manuscript and assortments of scrolls. The library categorized records based on their topic: court records, legal edicts, family records and details, imperial records and details. I needed to know the precise date of the marriage edict. From there, I could work backward to figure out just how my husband had changed from a young man into a murderous monster.

I beat down the inner thought reminding me of his recent behavior. It was probably a ruse, another test designed to force me to reveal a weakness he could later use against me. I had plotted to stay alive long enough to solve this mystery, and the mystery would not be solved while I sat idly by.

Locating the legal records, I went about six months back from the date of our marriage and started searching. After about twenty minutes, I pulled out a loose piece. Like all the parchments here, it was heavier than others, with a darker cream coloring.

It read:

> From this day forward, fully aware of the duplicitous, scheming, untrustworthy, and self-serving nature of woman, I, Shahryar al-Amin, decree thus: I will wed a new bride every night, and then, before she can use her womanly cunning to inflict harm on this Empire, execute her the following morning.

I noted the exact date and filed it away in my memory.

Now to see when the sultan married his first wife.

Examining the family records, I located my husband in the last set of pages in a bound manuscript. The list of marriages was long. I flipped back to the date immediately following the date of the edict. It was the second line of marriages. I frowned. He was married before this edict? The date of that first marriage was about five years prior to the law where he killed each wife. No wonder I didn't remember it—I was barely fourteen at the time, and not in a place to concern myself with politics and affairs of state.

So what happened during that first marriage? I found the registry entry with the woman's name on it: Jathbiyya.

> Jathbiyya, formerly of Byzantium, daughter of al-Zhir, ruler of Byzantium.
> Married to Sultan Shahryar al-Rashid on the fourth day of Shawal, two hundred years after the Hijrah.
> No issue.

Frowning, I read through the marriage record twice. It made no sense. During this marriage, our relationship with Byzantium had been strained. If the Sultan had married a Byzantine princess, wouldn't that have improved diplomacy?

I cross-referenced the entry for Jathbiyya. After two years of marriage, she had her own page in the archives.

Deceased on the eighth day of Jumada Al-Awwal, two
hundred and two years after the Hijrah. Cause:
Execution.

So he had killed every single wife thus far, with the exception of me. A
chill suffused through my body. I needed to learn what had happened if I
wanted any prayer of living through this marriage.

Byzantium. The conflict with Byzantium had ended a mere six
months ago—the date of the edict. The war had also begun, if I recalled
correctly, around the same date as Jathbiyya's death. Coincidence? As much
as I wanted to believe so, I studied too many mathematical theories to credit
something that exact as coincidence. And if Jathbiyya was from Byzantium,
it made sense that killing her would start a war.

I leafed back to Shahryar's entry. After Shahryar was the entry for his
brother—Muhammad. Muhammad's date of decease was almost exactly two
years after Jathbiyya's.

"Your Majesty." My guard emerged from behind a shelf, interrupting
my perusal. "Please, the hour grows late. We must return to your
chambers."

I rose, still holding the family record book. "Of course. Forgive me, I
lost track of time."

The exultation of being in a library again had stolen all sense of time
from me. I noticed with regret the sinking sun in the west-facing windows.
Glancing at the book, I started to return it to the shelf, then hesitated.
There was no guarantee of getting in here a second time. I knew this book
held some sort of answer, or at least a clue. Heart thudding, I pulled it
toward myself and followed the guard out of the library, book clearly in
hand. I could hear pounding in my ears as I waited for someone to approach
and stop me. No one seemed to notice.

As we made it out of the records area and down to the family wing, I
let out a breath I didn't realize I'd been holding. I'd done it. I'd purloined
the book.

Once back in my chambers, I hid the book among my other study
materials—thankfully, Duny hadn't taken everything. And the best place to
conceal something was in plain sight. Besides, the sultan never entered my
rooms without me there, and since most of the servants seemed to fear him,
I doubted any clerk would report the missing book before making a rather

extensive effort to find it on his own. And I only needed a few days with it to copy the important names and dates.

I would solve this mystery.

One Thousand and One Days

Chapter 8
Day 281: Sutaita

"I got the information on the war with Byzantium you wanted." Duny dropped a set of books onto the table with a thump. "It was hard to find. I had to wait until the librarian was distracted. It was in the section where they usually don't let women go."

I had confided to Duny about my findings in the Royal Archives. There was something with that first wife and the sultan's brother that was behind the bloodthirsty edict. If I figured out the connection, I would have a starting point for reasoning with the sultan, a potential solution.

Grabbing the tome on the top of the stack, I flipped it open. "Duny, the dates listed here are after Muhammad and Jathbiyya died." At least one of the records was wrong. And if they lied about the dates, what else had they lied about?

Dunyazade clearly thought the same as me. Her eyebrows knit. "Maybe their deaths caused the war. Maybe Byzantium sent assassins."

"It's possible," I murmured. Maybe Jathbiyya wasn't executed because of Shahryar's bloodlust, but because she helped assassins from Byzantium? Or had they targeted her as well? "But don't you think it's rather cold of the Byzantine emperor to assassinate his own daughter?"

"Jathbiyya was Byzantine?" Duny crossed over to glance over my shoulder at the book.

"Yes. Sorry I didn't explain that before. I didn't want to limit what you found. I believe it was an arranged marriage, meant to bring peace between the two nations." I tapped my finger against my jaw, thinking.

"Let's see what the cause of death for Muhammad was in the family history. If execution is a cover-up for assassinated, they'll have something similar for him." Duny retrieved the stolen manuscript from the Royal Archives and opened it to the bookmarked page. "Harun al-Rashid, cause of death: age. Muhammad...there is none." Duny's eyes widened and met mine. "Sutai? There's no reason!"

53

I frowned. "Are there any other entries with no cause of death?"

Duny flipped back through the book. "Illness. Battle. Age. Illness. Accident. No, they all have reasons."

"What about the public record?"

Duny set the family history down and searched through the stack of books. Locating the one she sought, she opened it. "That's strange."

"What?" I peeked over her shoulder at the open book.

"Here, it has his death listed as a casualty of war. See?" She pointed to the entry.

"The date's wrong, and different reasons for death are given." I read and re-read the entry, hoping I was just fuzzy-headed and reading it wrong. One error I could wave off as a mistake, as a clerical issue or communications breakdown. But two inconsistencies? With a sinking feeling, I knew I read the entry correctly. One of these records was wrong. But which one? And more importantly, why?

"There's our answer, if I can just figure it out..."

Duny grabbed my shoulder. "Sutai, be careful. There's a reason no one knows this secret."

"But why have incorrect records? Why would there be a discrepancy at all? Look, it's not as though the numbers were transposed or a mistake was made. This information is supposed to be checked and verified before it's published to the public." And a thought came to me that made me feel sick. "That means someone here knowingly gave the wrong information."

"But why?" Duny asked. "It just doesn't make sense. What sort of secret could giving the wrong date of death cover-up? It's such a stupid thing to lie about and so easy to disprove."

"Except that it isn't." My cheeks felt cold from lack of blood. "I had to pull rank to get into the archives in the first place. And with the civil war, executing a traitor would only prolong the fighting. And Byzantium declared war in the midst of all this. Maybe the sultan's hands were tied. He had to execute his brother in secret to avoid alienating Muhammad's supporters right before an external war."

"Why *did* Byzantium declare war?" Dunyazade mused. She returned to the war history and scanned over it. "According to this, Byzantium invaded. No reason is given, although the author asserts it was their ongoing desire to expand their borders."

"That still doesn't make any sense. Why not wait until Jathbiyya produced an heir, and offer to foster that heir to make the empire into a puppet state?"

"But you said Jathbiyya died before they invaded. Maybe her death caused it?"

"Then why not say that?" I argued. Although I was young, our family lived in the capital, and Father worked in the palace. If this woman had been of great renown or done great works or been beloved by the public, he would have told me stories about her, if only to inspire his daughter. I hadn't even heard of her until snooping in the records.

I ran through the timeline in my head again. Harun died and, on his deathbed, named Shahryar his heir. Civil unrest followed. And around the time of Muhammad's wife's death, the succession war. And then the war with Byzantium a couple years later. There was a string connecting these, something from the moment Shahryar assumed the throne that lasted until now.

Duny shrugged. "It appears you're right. This is the mystery. If you figure out why the secrecy and lies surround this, you'll probably figure out the edict. Did you steal a copy of that too?"

My shoulders slumped. "No. It was in a completely different folder. I can try and look at it again tomorrow."

"What if the sultan finds out?"

I reached across and put a comforting hand on hers. "I'm already a doomed woman. What do I have to lose?" It was so easy to speak those brave words. I'd been putting on a show for so long now that the false confidence came to me as easy as a breath of air.

Her head bent down, loose folds of her veil drifting across her face to hide the worry I knew was etched there. "I thought the sultan was being kinder. Better."

I walked to the window, fighting the tears gathering in my eyes. "Better than hating me with every bone in his body? Is that really an improvement?" I laid my forearms on the sill. "I'm a prisoner. In a pretty gilt cage with every bodily need met, but a prisoner nonetheless."

"Sutai..." Duny walked up behind me and gave me a hug. "It's barely been any time at all. You have to be patient and give it time. You've already lived how much longer than all the other brides?"

I shuddered. There were pages full of names, poor girls wedded, bedded, and killed the next day, in that family book.

But was it truly better to live imprisoned? Would death somehow give me the freedom I yearned for?

"I'll need to find the true cause of Muhammad's death." Better to focus on the concrete problem. Moping over my life wouldn't solve anything.

Sensing my change in mood, Duny withdrew. "I can try to look around in the history section again at the House of Wisdom."

I shook my head. "No, if you get caught in that section, you might lose access to the entire building. It's not worth it." I rose and straightened my shoulders. "I'll return to the archives here. I need to sneak that book back in anyway." I had only intended to keep it a few days. Thankfully, no calamities had occurred that would require adding information to the record, so hopefully, no one noticed it missing.

"Be careful, Sutai." Duny gathered her things. "I'll see what I can learn in the public sections and not risk admittance to the House of Wisdom. Until tomorrow, then?"

I nodded, then watched her flowing skirts fluttering with each step as she departed. With a sigh, I sank into a nearby cushion. The room was much better now than when I had first come. While the walls were still gold-enameled, the table was plain, with a basic linen runner as its only decoration. Plain muslin drapes hung across the window as well, instead of rich embroidered curtains. Most of the statues and other ornamentation were gone as well. It was a room meant for efficiency, comfort during work and study, but without excessive distractions and visual "noise."

After a moment, I forced myself up. I retrieved the stolen book from the table, tucked it under my arm, and left.

The scribes didn't even look up from their scribbling when I entered the archives. The same rushed man nodded to me and returned to filing and shelving items crammed onto a tiny hand cart. The tension I didn't even know I had slid out of me. I made my way toward the back section and replaced the book. Hopefully, no one had noticed its absence. And since, for now, there weren't nightly royal marriages, no one should need to update the records either. Or at least, that's what I told myself to bolster my courage. I considered trying to find the edict to read it again but decided against it as the hour was growing late.

I was on my way back out when the man stopped me. "Your Majesty, should I expect to see you here again in the near future?"

I thrust my hands behind my back so their trembling wouldn't give me away. "I apologize, sir, but I am uncertain how to address you—"

"I'm the head archivist, in charge of the creation, storing, and maintenance of all records for this palace, the ruling family, and the kingdom. You may call me Arash."

"Arash." I nodded. "I'm not certain when I'll be here next. All I want is to learn more about my new family. Unfortunately, the sultan is quite busy, so I've been left to my own devices in that regard." I felt certain Arash could hear the thudding of my heart against my ribs. I'd managed to bully him once, but this time, he'd disclosed his title and spoke with more authority. *Please, don't have told the sultan about this.*

Arash's eyes narrowed. "If you have historical questions about the dynasty, just ask me. I'm happy to help."

My heart beat a little faster. Should I ask? Could I take the risk? "I'm glad you offered. I actually did have a question. How did Muhammad—the sultan's late brother—die?"

Arash waved a hand. "Oh, that's easy enough. The Byzantine War. He was one of the many casualties."

My hands stopped trembling, stilling instead. I recalled what Dunyazade noted about the dates—and despite what was in the book I'd just returned, Arash gave the information from the House of Wisdom—from the common records. Of course it wouldn't be this easy. Arash either knew and was expected to play his part in concealing the truth, or didn't know and was duped like everyone else. The latter, to me, seemed highly unlikely, since he probably updated that very book. Which meant he did know, and now I was treading on very dangerous ground.

I met Arash's eyes, forcing my lips into a slight smile. "Oh, that makes perfect sense. Thank you."

"Anytime." Arash bowed slightly. "If that's all, I do have quite a bit of work to do here."

"Of course—sorry to keep you."

"Sultana, before you go." The scribe held out a hand.

I turned and pasted a smile on my face.

"Please make an appointment with me prior to any future visits here. I'd be happy to help you find any records you *need* to see." Arash turned back to his cart of tomes.

I maintained my smile and hopefully kept the fire of wrath burning inside me from showing. What I *needed* to see? Or what he would make sure I *wouldn't* see? I ambled away, deep in thought.

What if Muhammad was assassinated, and that was what started the war? Would a death like that be dishonorable and therefore excluded from the family records? My fists clenched in frustration. I couldn't check now that I had returned the book. I stalked back into my chamber and resumed pacing.

Think it through, Sutaita. If he was assassinated, and it was suppressed just as the conflict around Succession, the timeline worked. It would take time to draft and send a declaration of war to Byzantium. It would also explain the death of Jathbiyya—if she aided the assassin, she would be found guilty of treason and executed. It could also explain the sultan's edict: after she betrayed him, he lost trust in women. It worked perfectly.

But if it worked perfectly, why was there still a twinge of doubt in my gut?

Chapter 9
Day 283: Shahryar

Sutaita snored softly in her sleep. Over nine months now. With how things were going, I should try to conceive an heir with her. She seemed happy to simply be there for me. It was strange, something I wasn't used to. Then again, with the exception of Jathbiyya, I hadn't kept any woman around long enough to see what they were like.

Keeping Sutaita around permanently was still out of the question. But if I could stomach more than nine months, I could make it through the year or so it would take for her to birth a child.

But how to explain to that child why he had no mother? Something unfamiliar stabbed my heart.

I looked back at the sleeping woman. Would she tell our son the same stories? Would they capture his heart? I reached out a hand to stroke her hair—and yanked it back as she stirred.

She sat up, rubbing the sleep from her eyes. "Sorry, Your Majesty. I seem to have overslept."

I caught her hand in mine. "We were up later than usual last night. You're forgiven—this time."

If I hadn't been holding her hand, I wouldn't have known that a chill stole over her body at my words. A curse on this whole situation. She was so afraid of me, I couldn't even joke with her. That feeling I recognized—shame. I dropped her hand. "Let's get going, then."

During the prayers, I reflected on my marriage. It seemed that was all I did anymore when praying. Had my first marriage been this time-consuming? I couldn't remember. And anytime I thought of that—that woman—I saw red. I stole a glance at Sutaita, also kneeling in prayer. Best not think of Jathbiyya now. The last thing I needed was to be in that mood during breakfast.

I had come to enjoy the mornings with my wife. Her quiet confidence grated on me a little less. She didn't whine or prattle on and seemed to enjoy a quiet and calm companionship with me. I wished I could get closer to her—like she expressed in her parable—but something always held me back. And until I knew I could trust her, beyond any doubt, I wasn't about to let her close enough to know more of my secrets.

I thought about when I'd told her of Father's death. Some of the details were things omitted from the official statements and accounts. At the time, I'd regretted it. I felt certain she'd told her sister. That girl was in and out of here so much, I nearly offered her her own set of rooms in the family wing. But then I thought of Ja'far and how he would feel coming home to an empty house, and decided against it. Still, if Sutaita had told Dunyazade, they'd kept the story to themselves. Ja'far had made no mention of any improper remarks from Duny—and he would have told me if the girl had said anything—and no new rumors or speculation stirred through Baghdad. So, in this case at least, I'd chosen well to trust Sutaita.

Could I trust her more?

Prayers concluded, Sutaita silently followed me to the gardens. The birds chirped, the sound echoing off the palace walls. The cool rush of the nearby fountains soothed me. This truly was paradise. My stepmother had done well with her renovations.

"And how are you this morning, Sutaita?"

She looked up from her plate of dates and other fruits. "Well enough. Still a little tired. And you?"

Always so polite. Part of me wondered how she would be in the extreme of passion, when the ability to care about manners and propriety fled the mind. I should kiss her now. Kiss her and drive the façade of civility from her handsome head. But that painful clenching in my chest and tremor in my spine returned. No. I could not. Instead, I smiled. "I also am doing well."

The remainder of breakfast passed without words. Sutaita would gaze out at the various flowers, serenity smoothing the strength of her features and highlighting her femininity. While she was no beauty, I did enjoy studying her face, attempting to discern the minuscule changes that telegraphed her mood.

She bit her lip. I tensed. Something was amiss, something that made her afraid to speak. Ironically, I recognized it because it was how she seemed to feel most of the time. That strange feeling embedded itself in my chest again. I knew it was my fault, but I didn't know how to change it. I took a cleansing breath, keeping the motion minimal in hopes she wouldn't notice, and waited for her to speak.

"My lord, I wondered if I might have leave to depart the palace."

My eyes narrowed. "Why? Where would you go?" The question came out more harshly than I intended. What was wrong with me? *You don't want to be betrayed again.*

Her face smoothed, erasing emotion. Great, now we were back to this. I fought the desire to pound the table in frustration. If only she would drop the mask, drop the façade, and be genuine with me, show me I could trust her.

"Before I wed you, I would often visit the House of Wisdom to study. I wish to resume that practice, at least occasionally."

"No." It was out of the question. She must stay here so she couldn't plot against me. I tried, without success, to quash that reply. Damn it. And now that I'd denied her, I couldn't go back on it. What would she think of me then?

Pleading filled her eyes. "Your Majesty, we've been wed over nine months. Surely, you don't mean to confine me to the palace for the remainder of our lives?"

Her rebuttal only firmed my feelings. I was right—right to distrust her, right to make sure she didn't have a chance to breathe without my knowledge. I stood. "Yes, you are confined to the palace for the remainder of your life. And may I remind you that the duration of that life depends entirely upon me."

Her gaze wavered. "As you wish, Your Majesty. I had hoped—" She stopped short and swallowed. "Please excuse me."

I had scarce nodded when she stood and strode off. I wanted to bang my head against a wall. I had handled that terribly. I always reacted in anger. And how could she know why it scared me that she was educated, scared me that she was independent? Especially when that same intelligence and independence attracted me to her.

It was an out and out mess.

The rest of the morning passed rather uneventfully. I kept trying to focus on work, on running the enormous empire I'd inherited. But my thoughts kept turning to Sutaita.

Just before lunch, the head scribe, Arash, entered the throne room annex. He bowed, as expected.

"Rise," I commanded the man. "Can I help you?"

"Your Majesty, I am sorry to intrude. I felt compelled to seek you out. Your wife has visited the archives again."

I felt as if I'd been punched. "I must beg your pardon, Arash—could you say that again?"

He shifted from foot to foot. "Well, she first came a couple of months ago. I did not expect to see her, and as there is no policy in place, I did not feel comfortable turning away the sultana. But the family records went missing."

Heat bloomed in my chest. She had stolen from the archives. "The family records?"

"Yes, Sire. The records of births, marriages, deaths for the family. After she came, they were not in their proper place." Arash hesitated, opened his mouth, then stopped.

"Again, my deepest apologies. Are you informing me that my wife stole the family records from the archives?" I spoke very slowly, saying each word deliberately. The cold was sinking into my skin, funneling through my veins, icy rage that burned as it froze.

"Well, you see, that's the strange thing. She came again two days ago. And then the book was there again. I checked it; nothing was altered. So, perhaps she merely borrowed it?"

The ice turned to heat flowing through my veins as my rage burned hot. My head throbbed. "So you allowed her in a second time?"

Arash swallowed. "I did request that she make an appointment with me so I could seek you out and discern your thoughts."

Crimson rimmed the edges of my vision. How dare she! Poking around in my personal affairs? This was why I should have killed her. This was why I had this edict. "And she intends to sell whatever information she can find to the highest bidder?" I growled.

Arash bowed. "Forgive me, Your Majesty. I cannot say for certain. The reason she gave me was that you were consumed with your royal duties and didn't have time to share with her. She wanted to know more about you. However, she has mostly asked after your brother."

Fear froze the anger roiling through me. No. She could never find out that secret. She could never learn the truth of that awful day. I hadn't felt this afraid since...since my brother and first wife. Every inch of me throbbed with fear, rage, and something else, that same feeling from before that I couldn't name.

After a long moment to collect myself, I spoke again: "Thank you, Arash, for bringing this to my attention. Summon Ja'far for me on your way back to the archives."

Arash bowed. "As you wish." He rushed from the room.

I had to stop Sutaita from discovering the truth. Lives hinged on the information being kept secret. I'd already executed several guards. The only other person who knew the entirety of the matter was—

"Your Majesty, Arash informed me you desired counsel?" Ja'far's soothing tones broke through my racing thoughts.

"She's been visiting the archives." I gripped the sill of the inner window.

Ja'far crossed over to me. "Who has been visiting where?"

I whirled around to face him. "Your daughter! That sneaky, lying bitch is digging through the Royal Archives."

Ja'far's eyes flashed. "Your Majesty, while I understand your concern, striking out at me in anger is unlikely to help. Neither is insulting my family. I have done all I can to advise you impartially and been upfront with you when my relationship would color my judgment. Can you please take a moment, breathe, and speak with me about this as a man and ruler?"

Heat rose to my face. Of course he was right. Infuriatingly, Ja'far was always right. That's where Sutaita must have gotten her cold confidence from.

"Of course, Ja'far. Forgive me. I..." I paused, struggling to find the right words, "I'm worried." Scared witless, more like.

"Before we react hastily, why don't we explore some options, hmm?"

"She can't know the truth!" I snarled.

Hand resting on his chin, finger tapping his lip, Ja'far answered. "Well, that is one option. You tell her the truth."

"Unacceptable." I had worked too hard to keep it a secret. And hadn't this very course of events proved she was untrustworthy? If she had no reason to hide, why not just ask me?

Then I recalled what happened when she had asked for a simple outing mere hours ago, and that damn feeling from before—the one I didn't recognize and couldn't name—pricked my heart again.

"There is, of course, your edict. I would, I hope understandably, be put out if you chose that, but I must present you the option." Ja'far shrugged and sank into a nearby chair.

I considered it. Never seeing her face, never hearing her voice...and I wouldn't know how the story ended. Maybe if I waited, and once this one finished, I could do it. Somehow, she always got me to agree to another one. And now, we were three or four stories embedded. It would be months before it came to a conclusion. No, I couldn't do that. Besides, it was only a few months. Almost a year had already passed.

"If you will not—" Ja'far began.

"Cannot!"

"Tell her the truth," Ja'far continued, "then tell her the lie."

"She won't fall for the same lie I told everyone else. She's too cursed smart for that." And she was. That was the worst problem of all. If she'd been some simpering fool, I could trust at least in her idiocy, that she was incapable of plotting anything. *But if she wasn't smart, she couldn't tell you all those stories. If she wasn't smart, she wouldn't have shown you the passion for law and Allah hiding behind that cold mask, that sharp intelligence that keeps tempting, tempting...*

"Your Majesty, this situation is not as complicated as you are making it. She is your wife. Trust her with the truth as any husband should. If she honors that trust, return it with honor. If she doesn't, even I would not gainsay her execution. It's not as if you love her. What have you got to lose? I can personally attest that she knows none of your enemies and is not in contact with any unsavory or suspicious people. What's the worst that could happen?"

When Ja'far said, "It's not as if you love her," part of me wanted to fall to my knees and weep. My emotions were in such a state of turmoil, I scarce heard anything else after that. I pounded the sill. "She could go public with the information. She could undo the cover-up."

"Shahryar, she's a woman. You could easily discredit her."

That stopped me short. Ja'far was right. But I couldn't tell her the truth. Because deep down, I knew, in a way I could never articulate, could never explain, that if she knew who I truly was, she could never love me. And when did losing just the potential of her love become so terrifying?

That evening, I cornered Sutaita in the dining chamber. "You are not to go to the Royal Archives again."

She raised her chin. "Am I your wife?"

"Yes." What was she playing at?

"Then I am, by right, permitted access to every portion of this palace. You cannot forbid me the archives. However, if you wish to request that I not pursue any information, I will respect your request as your wife."

My chest tightened in anger, then relaxed. So that's what this was. She wanted attention. *They're all the same.*

"My wife," I said through gritted teeth, "I would appreciate it if you would direct any questions about family history to me. I will answer them happily."

Her lips pursed. "Very well. But I would rather share more of the story with you tonight, if it pleases you."

That statement calmed me, the calmest and easiest I'd felt all day. Despite everything, she would still share those stories with me. I smiled. "Yes, Sutaita, that would please me very much."

One Thousand and One Days

Chapter 10
Day 315: Sutaita

Despite the warm day, I shivered. The sultan's frosty eyes noted my movement and narrowed. He paused, about to speak, then thought the better of it and returned to his breakfast. I should have felt relieved, but my shoulders were as tight as ever.

I considered trying to talk to him, but the hard black gleam of his eyes dissuaded me. Despite his words to the contrary, he was not trying for closeness, for "more" at all. I was honestly surprised I was still alive. Sipping my coffee, I tried to relax my tight muscles. I was alive, here in the most beautiful garden, surrounded by fragrant blooms of roses and orchids.

"Why were you looking at the family records?" The sultan's deep voice shattered my thoughts.

We were back to this. He'd asked me every day for the past month. Part of me wondered if it was some sort of test. If he was waiting for one slip up, one change, to use to charge me with.

I set the cup of coffee down, trying to gain a moment to think. "I've tried to explain it to you. I'd like to try sharing it a different way this time." I took a breath, studying him. He didn't seem happy, but he didn't seem any angrier. "We didn't have a typical courtship. If I ever married, I expected to take time, meet my husband and his family in a Khastigāri. With only a day, none of this happened." My eyes found his, the harsh planes of his face softening. "You said you would try. Yet you keep secrets from me. Secrets of your past, secrets of your family. How can I be close to you with all these secrets between us?"

He slammed a hand down on the table. "I am not just any man, Sutaita. I am the sultan." He stood, his voice growing louder. "I cannot tell you everything. There are many matters you don't understand, things that must be secret—"

"I am a renowned scholar," I interrupted. "I can understand, and you can trust me to keep your secrets." He made me so angry. I was not a child, not a spy. And I had this gut feeling that if he'd just talk to me, I could figure out the puzzle, figure out the mystery, solve the riddle. Stay alive.

He shook his head. "Not this."

I thrust my chin out. We glared at each other from across the table. Duty won out. I looked down, acquiescing.

He left without another word.

Inexplicably, tears pooled in my eyes. I had been spoiled by my father, who shared all confidences with me growing up. *You forgot your place.* Except that this secret was the key to life. If I could learn it, understand it, I could solve the puzzle and not fear that every night would be my last. I dabbed the tears from my eyes with a napkin before leaving for my chamber.

In my room, a note awaited me on my study table. I opened it, noting the elegant hand. Written by a scribe.

> Sutaita,
>
> Please meet with me at your earliest convenience to plan a Pātakhti ceremony honoring your marriage to Sultan Shahryar. I apologize for the late organization of this event.
>
> Sincerely,
> Manoush

I re-read the letter twice, smiling when I saw that Manoush had listened to my request to keep things informal between us. She, at least, understood how I hated the ostentation and ceremony of the palace and my title. One thing bothered me, though. Manoush, who ran the palace kitchens and social events, had never asked my assistance in planning anything. And to have a Pātakhti so long after the marriage ceremony bordered on unthinkable. Was this Shahryar's doing? Did he think that he could go back and fix the sham that was our marriage by having these events now? Or was this his way of trying to apologize, trying to make things right?

With a sigh, I folded the letter and tucked it into my dress pocket. There was no time like the present to see Manoush.

The kitchens and scullery were in a rear wing of the palace, across the inner gardens. My duo of guards trotted after me, for once not trying to discourage me from leaving my rooms. As I neared the wing, I noticed a servant emerge from a hidden door in the hallway. I had wondered how the servants traversed the palace with food, and the ensuing dirty dishes, without being seen. Now I had my answer. I wondered if there was a hidden entrance in my rooms—or in the sleeping chamber. If there was one in the sultan's rooms, it more than likely led to the harems. I wrinkled my nose. While custom dictated the sultan keep a harem on hand for all courtiers' use, it was not the action of a devout Muslim.

I came upon the kitchen by following my nose. Many servants bustled about, stewing various meats and kneading soft mounds of dough.

A slightly heavy woman dressed in practical brown muslin approached. "Sutaita. Thank you again for meeting me on such short notice."

I smiled. "Of course."

The woman nodded. "I should have planned this weeks ago, but I am embarrassed to say, I got tired of planning feasts that were, in fact, funerals." Her eyes drooped. "It completely slipped my mind until the sultan sent a note down this morning."

With a strong force of will, I kept the smile plastered on my face to belie my racing thoughts. This morning? Did he really do this merely because I complained? Or was it to distract me?

"I have a small office further down the wing. It's not as hot or loud as the kitchens. Would you accompany me there?" Manoush ambled past me and out of the kitchen, not waiting for an answer.

I turned and followed her leisurely pace. "How long have you been running the kitchen?" I asked, careful to keep my tone light and friendly.

"Since before the war—Jathbiyya just wasn't interested, and none of the sultan's other marriages have lasted long enough for a wife to take over." She flashed me a smile that did not quite meet her eyes. "If you're interested—"

"Oh, no!" I stopped and reached a hand out to Manoush's shoulder to halt her. "I don't have the first idea of how to run a kitchen, let alone manage the entire palace."

Manoush let out a sigh. "That's a relief. It's a difficult job, but I do enjoy it." She continued down the hall, stopping after we passed two doors. "Here it is."

She opened the door to the messiest space I had ever had the misfortune to see. Books and scrolls were piled on every horizontal surface, occasionally spilling to the floor. Pens were scattered about, ink bottles left uncapped, and none of the candles were lit.

"Forgive the mess," Manoush said, pulling open drawers and lifting papers to search for something. "Arash is constantly on me to update things for the Royal Archives, but I just never seem to have the time." After a few more rustles, she retrieved a flint and set about lighting the candles.

An idea formed in my mind.

I started tidying up the papers, scanning them nonchalantly to see what they were. "So many documents. Whatever can Arash need from you?"

First candle lit, Manoush picked it up and began walking to others to light them. "Mostly names of servants, their families, and any incidents that occur when one is working. Arash cross-references anyone in the palace against political issues, violence, or other history that may indicate the person is a spy or assassin. Most of this is leftover from the perpetual weddings. We had a lot of extra help for all the feasts then, and it wasn't always the same people. And now that I am cutting back on staff since things have settled somewhat, I have to notate how and when they are released from duty. It's exhausting."

"I can't even imagine. I wish I could help."

The main desk was now somewhat organized.

"Oh, thank you for that. Now we can plan your Pātakhti! Please, have a seat." Manoush gestured to the simple wooden chair on the other side of her desk before sitting herself. "Did you have any particular day, guests, food, anything in mind?"

I shrugged. "Definitely my family. I suppose we should include influential sheikhs, make them feel as though they are part of the family."

A shrewd gleam sparked in Manoush's eye. "Smart choice. I'll check with Ja'far to see if there is anyone the sultan needs to win some favors from." She took down some notes on a blank piece of paper pulled from her desk. "And date?"

"I hadn't really thought about it. You should choose an auspicious day—you know what other events you need to plan around."

"That is very helpful, Your Majesty. If we're going to include sheiks, we'll need at least a month to send correspondence of the date and should give them ample time to make travel arrangements. Most of them will want to bring their wives, so it's not as simple as the sheikh coming for court. I think I'll need several months to prepare. Are you certain that's acceptable?

A warm smile grew on my face. Manoush was always considerate but direct. I nodded.

"Good." She took down another note on her paper. "I'll send around a message once everything is firmed up. Be sure to order a new dress for the occasion."

"Of course." I smiled. "And please, choose the menu as well. I have yet to be disappointed by a dish in my time here."

Manoush stopped taking notes. "Are you certain you're happy with me making all the arrangements?"

I swallowed the lump in my throat and tried to sound casual. "Absolutely. After seeing how overwhelmed you are, I couldn't bear to add to your work. Especially over choosing food for a party." I studied her face, which was soft and open. Taking a chance, I continued, "I would much rather help you with some of this administrative work so you can focus your energy on your staff and kitchen."

Manoush tapped her round chin with the feather of the pen. "Hmmm. Well, I do love planning the special events." She moved the pen aside and eyed the various piles on her desk, lip curling in disgust. "And I do hate paperwork." She extended her hand to me. "You've got yourself a deal."

I took the hand and gripped it warmly. "My pleasure. What can I do first?"

Dunyazade glanced up from her notes as I walked into my room. "There you are! Where have you been all day?"

Closing the door, I smothered a yawn. "Planning a Pātakhti and learning more about the administration of the palace."

Dunyazade frowned. "A Pātakhti? But that's supposed to happen the day after the marriage."

I rolled my eyes. "You mean the day I would have been killed?"

Her face colored. "Oh, right."

I sank into a nearby cushion with a sigh. "Sorry for being short with you. It's been a rough couple of weeks." And the sultan's constant interrogations weren't helping matters.

Duny smiled. "It's fine. I still don't understand why you're having the Pātakhti so late. At this point, why even have it at all? It's not as though you are cooking the food or need to set up your household."

Manoush's comment about the note from Shahryar confirmed my earlier suspicions. After my comment about not having the traditional parties and celebrations that made up a wedding, the sultan had decided to do what he could to address the lack. It was sweet, almost romantic—except that he still hadn't rescinded the edict that kept me living in fear every day of my life. It was as though he was scared about making an open, honest, romantic gesture—like it would compromise him in some way, weaken his ability to keep himself strong. The closest he had come was when he said he would try to make this like a real marriage. When I considered how little he had actually accomplished to that end, I didn't know if I should laugh or cry. *You said you didn't want a marriage or romance. You wanted to be a scholar.* Then why did the impersonal trappings of my marriage chafe at me so?

I couldn't tell Duny any of this. I didn't want her worried about the implications of my unhappiness—or that I even was unhappy. She was still combing all the records and histories in the House of Wisdom for hints and clues about the death of the sultan's first wife and brother. And I needed those answers more than I needed her sympathy.

"Well, I did gain an advantage. I'm helping Manoush with some of the household administrative work."

Duny straightened. "You mean—"

"I'll be in and out of those archives so much, Arash won't be able to tell if I'm getting any extra information." I flopped onto a nearby cushion. "But I will have to stay away from the family records, like I promised him."

"Finally, a breakthrough!" Duny leaped up. "This is huge! Especially since I'm getting nowhere fast at the House of Wisdom."

I nodded. "The answer is in those archives—I'm sure of it. Why else would Arash try to keep me out?"

Duny's head tilted to one side, considering. "He could be rather traditional and have a problem with you being there in general."

I shook my head. "That's not it. He has Manoush and several other women in and out of there for record-keeping purposes. Besides, if Muhammad was assassinated, it would say so. It wouldn't be blank... Something just doesn't add up."

"But who would know? We'd need a witness, someone to ask, or who might have recorded what really happened." Duny blew out a breath. "Where would we even begin looking for that?"

One of my guards ducked in and announced the evening meal.

My lips curled. "Duny, I think I know where to start looking." And luckily for me, it was nowhere near the family records, but instead in the staff records I'd just promised to help Manoush with.

Chapter 11
Day 372: Sutaita

"Tell me more about yourself, Sutaita. You spin these fabulous tales for me, but you never tell me anything personal."

As had become our tradition, we sat in the garden, enjoying the rushing sound of water fountains while breaking our fast. After that last time when I had tried to tie my poking in the archives to wanting to learn more about the family, he'd stopped interrogating me. It had taken a week or so for him to warm to small, pleasant bits of conversation during the meal, however. And now, over a year into this marriage, we had a pattern, a routine.

I colored slightly, embarrassed. "It is not my place to be forward, to advance myself. Allah is pleased with reserve, not boasting."

He chuckled. "That may be true, but I am not any man, I am your husband." He leaned forward, his eyes piercing mine. "Come, tell me about your life before this."

There was no avoiding this question. I swallowed, trying to calm my nerves. "My lord knows I am a scholar. I frequently visited the House of Wisdom built by your esteemed father—"

He waved this off, almost derisively. "Yes, yes, this I know. Everyone knows that. Gossip about Vizier Ja'far's daughter and her bookish ways have been known for quite some time. No, this won't do. Tell me a secret—something private, something only your family knows."

My mind raced. A secret? I had done nothing but try to be open since being married. I knew he mistrusted the female gender, so I strove to be as honest and clear as possible. Why would he want to know something personal? Was this a resumption of his attempts for "more," for closeness? I'd kept my word, and while I helped Manoush catch up with her paperwork and filed it in the archives, I'd kept noticeably far away from the section that housed the family records. On the rare occasions where something I had needed to be filed in that area, I gave it to Arash instead of filing it myself. It had made further research with Dunyazade difficult, if not impossible. Anytime I got to peek at the guard rosters, however, I'd done my best to read and memorize as much as possible. I still hadn't found anything even remotely resembling a clue.

He noticed my furrowed brow and laughed aloud. "So hard to confide in me, wife?" Then his face became serious. "Or do you have too many secrets to choose from?"

With that, he returned us to our emotional battlefield. Once strange, this territory now felt like home. It seemed a constant cycle, him doubting me, me reassuring him, him testing me, then realizing that whatever his previous experiences were, I was not like other women.

"My lord, I have no secret that I can think of. That is my difficulty."

The tightness around his eyes and mouth disappeared. "No personal details? Even something small, like a favorite toy or pastime from your childhood?"

I bit my lip. "Why so curious?"

"We are married. Over a year now, if memory serves. And I find myself unable to really describe you. I don't really know you. I know Sutaita the storyteller. I know Sutaita the scholar. But who are you inside? What makes you want to live, makes you feel alive?" Shahryar leaned in close. "Would it help if I confided in you first?"

Unable to speak, I nodded.

He leaned back. "I love this empire, its people, making everyone's life better, richer, fulfilled. I never wanted this position, but accepting my responsibilities and rising to the challenge of leadership—it satisfies me in a way I never thought possible. It helped when—" His eyes rounded in sorrow, while his lips tightened in anger. "Well, never mind that."

I pasted a smile on my face. He was about to tell me something—an important clue to the mystery. I must not let my curiosity show. "Thank you. I never knew how much it meant to you—being sultan." My eyes dropped to the nervous fingers twisting the linen napkin under the table, away from his gaze. "You are rather secretive as well, you know."

He smiled back at me, his eyes sparkling in the morning light. "I am trying, Sutaita. For you, I am trying."

And, for the first time, he really was. How could I match such intimacy? For him, as closed as he was, the admission was incredibly personal. I thought about what I could share that would mean the most, show how much he had risen in my regard.

"Scheherazade. My father's name for me. It's a personal name." I met his eyes, blushing.

I couldn't quite decipher the expression on his face. "That is an...interesting nickname. There must be some additional significance?"

I willed my voice to remain steady. "He says that when he first became a father, he feared that he would be trapped. But as he taught me and watched me grow, he realized that it was the opposite. He was now free, free to pursue his dreams, knowing that his family line would continue, somehow. Knowing that his memory would live on—in me." I shrugged, feeling my cheeks burn with embarrassment. "He always said this, but I didn't understand him until recently." *Until my own imprisonment*, but I daren't say that.

Shahryar gazed at me silently. The world seemed to still, as though a single second stretched into hours. I had truly bared my soul to him. The freedom my father named me for was the chief thing I ached for. I looked away from him. The open horizon beyond the wall of the garden beckoned. My eyes watered slightly, threatening to overflow. The confinement in the palace, with a husband I didn't want, who didn't want me...I felt the need for freedom more acutely than ever.

Shahryar's eyes narrowed slightly, studying me. "More, I think, than just your father's feelings, hmm?"

For the first time ever in his presence, I lost all emotional control. The tears that had welled up in my eyes took over, a single drop leaking out and streaking down my face. I looked down. "If my lord will excuse me." I barely waited for his assent before bolting out of the garden.

It was too much. Exactly three hundred and seventy-two days. I knew because I counted each, feeling them as surely as if I'd carved a notch for each in my skin. I barely made it into the family wing before I sank to the floor and let the tears consume me. Thankfully, because the servants had learned my habits and took this time to tend to other duties, I had the wing to myself. No one witnessed my control evaporate.

It hurt so much, so much more than I had anticipated. And as time had stretched on, Duny had scaled back her visits. She was the only true company I had.

This constant emotional battlefield—how much longer could I endure it? My nerves were fraying and shot, and I was no closer to an answer now than I had been a year ago. I cried myself out, then, wiping the tears from my eyes, made for my room and the privacy it offered.

Later that afternoon, he arrived unexpectedly at my chamber. I sat in a corner, working on a mathematics problem. Successoral calculations were my specialty, so working on them helped to calm my feelings. I glanced up and stood as quickly as I could once I realized he was there.

"You said you would visit the House of Wisdom?"

I struggled to breathe. "Yes, my lord."

"Well then, let's go. You can show me what you did there."

Elation filled me. I couldn't believe my ears. I was allowed to leave the palace? *Keep calm*, I told myself. One emotional outburst for the day was more than enough. My heart raced as I followed him out of my chamber and into the palace courtyard. He extended a hand to me. I took it and climbed into the waiting palanquin with his assistance. He entered after me. After closing the beige curtains, he pulled me toward him so I reclined onto his chest. He gently rubbed my arm with his hand and kissed my forehead lightly. I stiffened, unused to the physical contact.

He whispered into my ear, "I have not been to the House—since Father's death."

I looked over at him, eyebrows raised in question.

"It was too hard. He had such hopes for it—and I had believed that my brother was to be sultan. I loved it but knew that I could never hope to advance the knowledge contained within." He sighed, squeezing me closer to him. "And now you, lovely Scheherazade."

I started at his use of my nickname.

"You are teaching me how to find freedom—from the past."

It was as if time itself froze. He had never said anything truly kind to me until that moment. And even more, to think that I had helped him move past whatever demons drove him—it was nothing I had ever planned for, nothing I had ever desired. My stomach churned but, surprisingly, not in fear, as I was accustomed.

I noticed the streaks of honey gold in his dark eyes and a softness in them I'd never seen before. I felt his breath, warm and sweet, like dates and camel's milk, on my face. And a yearning came over me. I found myself imagining what it would be like to kiss him.

The din of people trading in the bazaar swelled as the palanquin wound through the streets of Baghdad. Through the translucent flutter of the curtains, I noticed crowds disperse, yielding the right of way to the sultan as a guard called out. It brought me to my senses. *Don't forget—he will kill you. You must never let down your guard.*

"I had planned to be a scholar—never marry, only learn and teach until I had learned everything I possibly could." My eyes met his. "My sister is the one who wanted a husband, a family."

Holding my gaze, something in him seemed to soften. "And now? What do you plan now?"

I couldn't look away. Something connected me to him, drew me to him. It was like nothing I had ever experienced. It was exhilarating...and terrifying. Was it possible that I was wrong—that he was changing, was no longer the evil despot who had married a new woman each night and killed her the following morning? There was no hint of the anger, the rage I'd seen glimpses of, in those soft, coffee-colored eyes. I swallowed and answered him, "I don't know. With everything that's happened, I never stopped to think about being a wife or continuing to be a scholar. And now...I never dreamed that I could have both."

His eyes sparkled with that rare something they began to show when he beheld me. "And I never dreamed of finding freedom in a woman."

One Thousand and One Days

Chapter 12
Day 451: Shahryar

Nearly four months had passed since that first trip to the House of Wisdom with Sutaita.

I didn't know what to do with myself.

My days had settled into a comfortable routine: prayer and breakfast in the morning with Sutaita, hold court during the day, and accompanying Sutaita every three days or so to the House of Wisdom. She never expected to go and always appreciated the opportunity to exchange her old study materials for new books and scrolls. And part of me liked this routine. It felt comfortable—just like the clothing in Sutaita's parable.

And with the distraction the House of Wisdom offered, I hadn't received any new reports of clandestine visits to the archives. I knew of her assisting Manoush, and it pleased me. She seemed to understand that Manoush needed the responsibility of the household, and instead homed in on how her strengths complimented Manoush's by handling the paperwork. Arash told me that Sutaita had scrupulously avoided the family section, going out of her way to avoid even the suggestion of impropriety or betrayal of her promise.

Ja'far smiled at me as he approached. "You seem well-rested and content this morning."

We clasped hands in greeting. "Indeed, I am. Despite last night's suspenseful story, I find myself eagerly looking forward to the next saga tonight."

Ja'far's smile did not quite reach his eyes. "I am glad you find your wife pleasing, my lord."

Dropping his hand, I continued down the hall, a storm covering my previously happy mood. The shadow of my past—the killing, the edict—ruined everything. I was having a nice morning before Ja'far's constant worry clouded it.

But I couldn't change things—couldn't take that chance. After all, there were those secret trips to the archives. Sutaita was just as much a woman as all the others—just as secretive and just as likely to one day betray me. Just because she appeared to be keeping her promise now didn't mean she always would.

The thought of her death, however...

"Ja'far, I would like to take a personal day." I stopped short. Whirling about, I barely caught his startled expression before he smoothed his face into its mask of stoicism. It was not the first time I noticed the similarities between him and his daughter. *Is she still alive because she reminds me of him? Of a trusted adviser—nay, a friend—whom I love dearly?*

Ja'far's voice broke into my thoughts. "Of course, my lord. I will dismiss the court immediately. Do you require my attendance afterward?"

And if I do? Will you sit and watch me play the part of happy husband with your daughter? I stopped those thoughts in their tracks. Sutaita and Ja'far were too similar. I began to hold him in the same distrust I held her. That would never do. Was I going mad?

"My lord?" Ja'far asked.

"No, please, enjoy a day off as well. You've earned it."

A small smile ghosted across Ja'far's face. "Yes, my lord. Until tomorrow." He bowed and continued down to the courtroom.

I retraced my steps and returned to the family wing. Murmuring female voices sang through the stone walls. Sutaita and Dunyazade were already deep in conversation. I entered the room and announced myself.

Dunyazade rose with a blush. Was it my imagination, or did Sutaita pale? What were they up to?

"And how go your studies today?" I sank, unbidden, into a nearby cushion.

Dunyazade cleared her throat, then started coughing.

Sutaita tucked back an imaginary lock of hair behind her ear. "Very well, my lord. To what do we owe the pleasure of your company?"

"Does a man need a reason to dote upon his wife?" I waited for her response.

She shook her head.

"Well, then, what are you studying today?"

Dunyazade glanced at her sister.

Sutaita, ever icy, ignored her sister. "Dunyazade has only just arrived, my lord. We were merely gossiping when you arrived."

That was when I knew I had her. Manoush had told me that the sultana was remarkably reserved, with none of the silliness she's witnessed in the previous girls I'd married. I'd never seen Sutaita even make an offhand comment about someone.

I stood. "Dunyazade, I must ask you to excuse us."

"Yes, my lord," she squeaked before gathering a few books and darting out of the room.

I caught Sutaita's eyes and held them. "Now, Sutaita, the truth. What were the two of you discussing?"

Her lower lip quivered—barely, but it did move. Still, she said nothing.

"Answer me." The low growl of my voice surprised even me. I was familiar with icy rage, where my blood felt as though it froze as anger blinded me. This was nothing like that. Instead, hot fire shot through my veins.

Sutaita swallowed. "I do not wish to tell you a lie, my lord. But I do not wish to share the topic of my conversation with you."

"You would keep secrets from your husband?" Now the cold anger emerged.

"Do you not keep secrets from me?" she answered.

I turned away and strode toward the open window. "That's different."

"Is it?"

I pivoted to face her again. Not one trace of emotion colored her face. Damn her. How did she always do this?

"And what secret do I keep from you that you want to know?"

Sutaita sat down and smoothed her skirt. "What happened to your first wife?"

No. I would not—could not—share that. She already thought me a monster for murdering dozens of other women. And she was right. But as long as she didn't know the extent of my humiliation, my vulnerability—I would be safe.

It took me a minute to get the words past my now constricted throat. "Please, Sutaita. Anything but that."

After a moment that felt like an eternity, she nodded. "Very well. Then what happened to your brother? The truth, not whatever story was concocted to protect the empire."

I studied her. No trace of pride or arrogance marred her handsome face. Impassive, she sat, waiting for my response.

"Why?" I whispered.

Her face softened. "Because until I know the truth, we cannot truly be husband and wife. Because I want to understand you, not as a sultan or a husband or a leader, but as a man. As a friend. As a companion."

My heart felt as though it had been stabbed. "Was that why you were poking around in the archives?"

"Yes." Not a second of hesitation. She was being honest.

"And if I don't tell you?"

The silence stretched between us, slowing time. Seconds crawled on.

"That is your choice, my lord. But until you confront whatever makes you keep secrets, whatever led you to kill dozens of women, whatever still haunts you, you won't truly live. Whatever happened has already killed you."

Her words felt like a slap in the face and a punch in the stomach at the same time. Curse her, she was right. I stood up and stalked over to the window. The smell of jasmine and oranges floated in from the nearby trees. I breathed it in, trying to calm my racing pulse. I turned my head and studied Sutaita. She sat on her cushion, eyes as hard as stones. Maybe I could share some—not the whole of it, but enough to sate her thirst for knowledge.

"You asked about my brother."

Her eyes softened. "Yes, my lord."

I took a deep breath. "I told you how he imprisoned me and started a fight for the throne."

She nodded.

"Well, I got over my initial hesitation and joined the fray. With the testimony of Tahmores, I had great success..."

Despite the steady losses Muhammad suffered and the abandonment of the sheikhs, he had held out stalwartly at our family seat. I sent several messengers, pleading for him to come and talk to me. All had gone unanswered. The last one never returned, and I believed him dead. But here, a few months later, Muhammad arrived in Baghdad. I hoped to speak with him, to mend the rift between us. However, instead of seeking me out, he demanded—*demanded*—a royal audience.

My brother arrived with as much fanfare as he could contrive to summon. He rode atop a gleaming destrier, accompanied by a contingent of soldiers in shining armor. A paltry group of followers marched behind the soldiers, their patched and dirty clothing reflected the true state of affairs for Muhammad. The sheikhs coming to my support had allowed me to blockade and embargo the family seat. Unfortunately, the people there were suffering—many had chosen to escape to the city and make a new life here in Baghdad. By the looks of things, he brought almost every last resident of the family seat with him in some capacity.

He was escorted under armed guard into the throne room, where I sat waiting. The residing sheikhs also sat assembled, bearing witness with their silent stares. My guards had refused to allow even one retainer to accompany Muhammad into my presence. The guards and camp followers had been forced to wait outside the palace walls, under heavy observation.

Muhammad sauntered in, confidence encasing him like a cloak. He stopped before the throne and merely nodded. A gasp of shocked surprise echoed from the attendants. Protocol demanded that he at least bow. Tahmores, standing on my right, tightened his mouth but did not comment. Ja'far was standing a little ways behind him but had schooled his face to emptiness. A necessary skill, that.

Watching him after all we'd been through, seeing him after we'd both sent hundreds of our own countrymen to their death rather than settle this face to face, I seethed in anger.

In light of the situation, I chose silence. I would wait for Muhammad to state his case and move from there. The silence stretched and filled the room until the very absence of sound seemed to echo from the rafters. I almost thought I heard my heartbeat thudding and thrumming in the tense air.

He finally took the bait and broke the silence. "Brother, I have come to announce my engagement."

Silence. No threat, no surrender, and certainly no apology. A reaction from me must wait.

"I am to marry in an auspicious time, three months from now." His pompous attitude now seemed a thin veneer. For the first time since his arrival, I spied the lines of tension and worry around his eyes. Did he honestly think that I would forgive and forget him attempting to kill me? Him imprisoning me, instead of sitting down and talking like family? Demanding this very public arena to finally speak with me after ignoring and killing my messengers?

Despite my best intentions, I felt my inner anger heat my face. Pressing my lips firmly together, I resolved to maintain my silence. I focused instead on breathing, on trying to soothe the burning sensation of my face. The second silence stretched to fill the room again. The air seemed to thicken, making it hard to breathe.

Muhammad looked around, confusion dawning on his face. "Don't you have anything to say? I am your brother!"

I gazed at him steadily. He met my eyes but, after a second, wavered and looked down. His haughtiness dissolved like honey in tea. He abruptly turned to leave.

"Wait." I rose from the throne. He turned and was forced to look up into my towering face. "Besides announcing your engagement, are there any other statements you wish to make to the throne?"

His eyes narrowed. He looked at the assembled sheikhs, glaring at a few with outright hatred. Lips pursed, he turned back to me. "I formally renounce my claim to the empire. Satisfied?"

Not trusting myself to speak, I nodded. I raised my hand, signaling the attending scribes to begin taking down my words. "Our brother has seen the error of his ways and has formally renounced the source of division within this country. Let us determine now to move forward, in peace and prosperity, as family, like Allah intended."

The room buzzed as sheikhs began speaking with each other, confused about my edict. Muhammad's actions demanded death under the law, did they not? How could I justify suffering a traitor to live? And acknowledging the same traitor as family?

"Allah would never accept the condemnation of a brother—is it not Shari'a law that he receive an equal inheritance to mine? Therefore, we will forgive our brother his madness following the tragic death of our father."

Nobody's shock matched that of Muhammad's. His eyebrows raised, his mouth moved as if to question me, but no words formed.

I approached him and said softly for only his ears, "I wish this conflict between us ended. I will gift you with land in celebration of your nuptials. Please see this as a gesture of goodwill, with the desire that we see ourselves as family first, rulers second."

With that, I left him.

Muhammad resided in the palace while I finalized bestowing land and titles on him to commemorate his impending marriage. The court was abuzz with news of our reconciliation, and I hosted several parties and dinners to celebrate.

Sutaita's gaze never wavered as I told her the story. "So you were reconciled with your brother."

I nodded. If I didn't voice it, it wasn't a lie, was it?

She mulled this information over. "I confess, it makes me wonder what caused his death. When I looked in the family record, there was no reason listed. A tragic omission for your beloved brother, no?"

Curse her and her cleverness. I clenched fists hidden in the folds of my tunic so she couldn't see. "Sutaita, there is more to the story, but please, believe me when I say that I can't tell you."

She nodded, eyes grave. "And please believe me when I tell you that until you can tell me, I cannot tell you everything either. Trust goes both ways, my lord."

I stiffened, an angry retort on my tongue. Then I remembered why I was here. I hadn't come to question her, to intimidate her. I'd asked for a personal day to spend time with her because I couldn't keep her off my mind. When I closed my eyes, her face, with the cool reserve that once I'd abhorred, filled my imagination. I noticed how, when she told stories and when we visited the House of Wisdom, light and energy suffused that face, making her eyes sparkle and the strong angles of her jaw and nose soften.

I had a choice, just like I'd had with Muhammad: to put family before empire. I'd tried to do that with Jathbiyya. It had blown up in my face. But with Sutaita...

"One last question, then, my wife. Why did you marry me?"

She paled. "Does it matter? I chose, and I am here."

"It matters to me. Please, I will let my first question go if you will answer this one." I hated begging, and why did I feel so weak right now?

She swallowed and looked away. "Dunyazade. I had to try to save her. Had to try to live long enough that she wouldn't be next."

Family. She'd offered herself for family. For her sister. She'd accepted, knowing full well that death awaited her. And she'd put family before her own life.

"Tell me, wife. How would you like to spend this day? I am at your disposal."

The sparkle in her eyes somehow made everything worth it.

One Thousand and One Days

Chapter 13
Day 557: Sutaita

What didn't he tell me?

The question kept swirling through my thoughts. Shahryar made it sound like he and Muhammad had reconciled, like the succession conflict ended the enmity between them. But if all was well, why the cryptic entry in the family records? And why didn't the timeline match up?

I took a sip of coffee and tried to focus on the book in front of me. The words blurred as my thoughts returned to Shahryar's puzzle. Pursing my lips in disgust, I closed the book. Studying wasn't happening today.

Instead, I retrieved a small piece of parchment: my notes of the clues so far. The last entry summarized Shahryar's story. Where it fit into the larger portrait, I knew not. And how women and marriage fit into this scheme was still unknown.

I scowled at the parchment. Somehow, I had to find out about Jathbiyaa. I tapped my nails against the polished almond wood of the desk. Then it hit me. There were no women on my list. Shahryar spoke of Muhammad's marriage, but he hadn't said what happened to Muhammad's wife. But who would know about her?

I bit off a curse. I hadn't even thought to look up her name when I checked the family records. After years of being overlooked, merely for being a woman, I had committed the same wrong. Surely that was the key I needed.

But that information was probably only in the family records—the records I'd promised Shahryar not to look at.

You could always ask him.

I dismissed that idea almost as quickly as it sparked. I'd tried the patiently waiting route for over three months now to no avail. And asking him right out? Shahryar's temper was uncertain at the best of times—the risk was too great. There had to be another option.

A servant entered my room. "Excuse me, Your Majesty?"

I jumped. I'd been so lost in thought that I hadn't heard the servant approaching. Panic washed over me. She mustn't see my notes. "Yes?" I tucked the incriminating parchment under a few other pages.

"Manoush needs you for the final touches for the Pātakhti, if you please." The servant made a small bow and gestured for me to accompany her.

I smoothed my face and stood. "Of course."

Words cannot describe how grateful I was that the Pātakhti was almost done. What was supposed to be a simple celebration after the marriage had transformed into a nightmare of planning, decorating, and coordinating. Usually, a Pātakhti was nothing more than a small party where the family gave gifts to the newlyweds. A Pātakhti for the sultan and his wife, however, involved all the sheikhs and their families. The court had been relatively quiet since our marriage—something about it lasting for more than a day. The sheikhs were more than ready for a grand party, so a grand party we would give them. This utterly destroyed the hope of having it a couple of months after we began planning, but Manoush hadn't seemed to mind.

I made my way to the kitchens, where Manoush tended to be at this time of day.

"Sutaita—there you are." Manoush wiped her large hands on a cloth and approached. The spices of baking permeated the kitchen: cloves, cinnamon, and vanilla. Manoush waved me over to a tray of desserts. "Please let me know which one you prefer."

I studied the tray of sweets. An assortment of ranginak with green shavings, shiny glazed bamieh smelling of rosewater, baklava dripping with walnuts and honey, cream-colored gaz dotted with pistachios, and saffron cakes dusted with cinnamon covered the tray. There were easily a dozen choices. This would not be pleasant. I normally abstained from desserts, except for special occasions.

"Manoush, is there one that the sultan prefers?" I secretly hoped to take the easy way out and select his favorite.

"Hmm." Manoush surveyed the tray. "If I recall, he's always been partial to honey cakes." She winked at me. "But it's your first and only Pātakhti, so you should choose your favorite."

I attempted to smile. "No, let's go with the honey cakes, then. I would see to his pleasure before mine, especially since I am not partial to sweets."

Manoush patted my hand approvingly. "Such a devoted wife. Certainly better than the last one."

Was this my chance? My way in? I swallowed and willed my voice to stay even. "Last one? Surely you didn't have time to plan a Pātakhti if they were only married a day."

Manoush picked up the tray and started toward the back of the kitchen, where the servants' food was left. They would get their pick of the samples now that I'd decided what I wanted for the party.

"No, not any of those. They hardly count." She shook her head. "I meant his first wife. The Byzantine girl."

I hid my hands in my sleeves so Manoush would not see my fingers clenching. "Oh? She wasn't devoted to the sultan?"

Manoush set the tray down with a snort. "Anything but. I knew that girl was trouble from the start. But no one listens to Manoush." She strode past me and headed out of the kitchen.

I followed her, justifying it by telling myself she hadn't dismissed me yet. Manoush was an untapped resource—and she saw everything. She was also a notorious gossip. I usually just nodded along with her ramblings, but if I could deftly turn her stream of words to the information I wanted, I might learn something, something important—and with no one the wiser.

"It was right after the sultan and his brother reconciled. With the succession settled, all the neighboring nations sent envoys—spies, if you ask me—and the sultan let them stay here in the palace," Manoush continued as she made her way down the hall, the floor echoing with the thuds of her heavy footsteps.

I made a noise of disapproval.

Manoush shrugged. "I was told it was custom to host these envoys. But they were spies. Why else would Byzantium send a woman?"

"They sent a woman alone?"

"No, as part of the group. Most of them sent a woman—wanted to snare the sultan, make an alliance through marriage. The sultan was far too young, too new to being a ruler. I've been serving in the palace under three sultans: Shahryar's father, Harun, and his grandfather too. These men have to learn how to be a ruler before they can be a husband. If they marry too young..." Manoush's voice trailed off as she turned off the main hall, shaking her head.

"Anyways, that one from Byzantium caught his eye. Caught all the mens' eyes, if you know what I mean." She turned to look at me, a knowing gleam in her eye.

I nodded and hoped I masked my discomfort. The prevailing rumor in the palace was that I'd ensnared the sultan with my feminine wiles. Some less than compassionate sheikhs even suggested that I'd studied foreign texts to learn how to best please a man and employed my knowledge to keep myself alive. If Manoush believed that, far be it from me to disabuse her.

I turned toward the open door, keeping an eye on the hallway. It wouldn't do for someone to overhear this confidence. "She must have been special to outshine that many rivals."

"Well, yes. She was rather magnificent." Manoush selected a paper and held it to her chest. "It was her smile. It dazzled the whole court. She sat next to the sultan during dinner, laughing and smiling that infectious smile." Manoush shook her head and brushed past me, leaving her office.

I followed. "A whirlwind romance, then?"

Manoush snorted. "No. The sultan was too worried about his brother's marriage, bleeding heart that he is."

I fought to hide a scowl at that. Bleeding heart, the sultan? Was Manoush even speaking of the same person with whom I spent each night?

"Anyway, she remained at court for nearly a year before a treaty was agreed upon and the engagement announced. The sheikhs of the court took to her instantly. Everyone liked her."

"Except you, of course."

Manoush smiled. "Right. Except me. But no one listens to me, so there you have it." She picked up a piece of chalk and began copying the information on the parchment to the menu board.

"Thank you for your time, Manoush. It's been…enlightening. Did you need me for anything else?"

Manoush shook her head, intent on her copying. I gave her a small nod and slipped out of the kitchen.

I wondered what had happened during that year. A year was a long time for a political marriage. Usually the treaty negotiations preceded the marriage, but once marriage was agreed upon, both parties wanted the act completed quickly, lest one of the parties die or an impropriety be discovered before the marriage took place.

And Manoush's information, while helpful, didn't really explain much of anything. I already knew Jathbiyya was Byzantine, already knew that she had somehow married Shahryar. That it was, at least from outside appearances, a political marriage meant nothing.

But what if it wasn't political? The thought made me halt dead in my tracks. The long courtship, the less than stable political alliance, the apparent fallout causing no honorable notation surrounding her death all pointed to some sort of agenda. Assuming politics was easy: she was a spy, the sultan suspected and thus took his time before marriage, the alliance was shaky anyway given the history between the two nations, and when one side wanted war, the spy got caught and executed. Easy.

But where in that easy description did the murder of dozens of new young Persian brides make any sense?

I was so lost in thought, I nearly plowed someone over as I turned the corner. "My apologies," I murmured as I bowed.

"Sutaita, what are you doing?"

It was Shahryar. I tried to swallow the lump forming in my throat. "Manoush had questions about the Pātakhti. I've just returned from the kitchens." I dared a glance at him.

He was rubbing his shoulder, presumably where I'd charged him. "Good. So you can tell me which cake you chose."

My lips curved in a smile. "Certainly, my lord. As soon as I finish telling you the tales of Sinbad the Sailor."

His eyes met mine, a spark in them I'd never noticed before. "And tell me, dear Scheherezade, will that happen before I die?"

My voice caught in my throat. I forced my lips to stay curled in a smile.

"Well, I hope you chose a good dessert. I told Manoush to let you choose, so you could have your favorite."

My jaw nearly dropped. He wanted me to have something I wanted? Maybe I could take a chance. Maybe I could just ask him.

"My lord—I—that is, if you have some time—"

He studied me. "Are you all right, Sutaita?"

I felt my cheeks flush. "Yes, my lord. I just have something to ask you. I know the question to be impudent and impertinent, but it weighs so heavy on me." I met his eyes. Not hard and cold. Maybe this would work.

"By all means, Sutaita. Ask me your impertinent question. But might you ask it in the gardens so I can recline?"

I nodded. "Of course, my lord." I was extremely fortunate today. Not only had Manoush been willing to talk, but Shahryar seemed in a pleasant mood and willing, for once, to indulge me. I followed him out into the gardens.

He selected a glade near a fountain, where the sweet perfume of flowers drifted on the slight breeze. "Now, Sutaita, what burdens you?"

I took a breath to calm my nerves. "My lord, I want to know more about you—including your first marriage. That's why I was looking in the archives. I've tried to forget about it, truly, but today with the Pātakhti, all I could think about was that something went wrong there and how I wanted desperately to make sure I did not repeat her mistake."

Silence stretched between us. I kept my face averted, afraid of what I might see if I looked at him.

Finally, he cleared his throat. "I must admit, I did not expect that question, Sutaita." He sighed. "But I suppose you do have a right to know."

I peered up at him. How could he have changed? I'd expected a refusal at best, like he had every time I'd tried to glean this information from him. Mayhap the storytelling had another side effect. As I told him stories, the rule of reciprocity bound him to do the same. Was that all I needed to do? No sneaking around, no hunting for the truth?

A haunted look filled his eyes. "I assume you know she came from Byzantium, part of a diplomatic envoy?"

I nodded.

"Well, our marriage was more than just a political agreement. I loved her, Sutaita. Loved her more than anyone else. Her smile...it was akin to the flare of flint striking steel, sparkling and exciting. I could marry her and secure our border—I wanted to marry her for my own reasons." He shifted, trying to ease the discomfort in his heart by increasing the comfort of his body. "She remained at court for nearly a year before a treaty was agreed upon and the engagement announced. In that time, I did grow to love her. There was no sadness, no heartache, no difficulty that a few minutes with her effervescent happiness could not cure.

"After a couple years of marriage, however, it became clear that there was a problem..."

Shahryar

I approached her in the gardens on the second anniversary of our marriage.

"And how are you today, sweet?"

She looked up at me and smiled, but I noticed that her eyes were rimmed with red. "I'm all right." She took a breath. "I regret to inform you I still am not carrying your child." She bit her lip and looked away.

I went and sat next to her. A long moment stretched between us. I will admit, I was disappointed. There was nothing I wanted more in the world than to start a family with her. But her welfare was more important than my feelings. I tentatively put an arm around her shoulders.

She responded by turning into my chest and sobbing. I stroked her hair, making soothing noises.

"I'm sorry, Shah…I didn't mean to cry like that."

"It's okay, sweet." I reached out and lifted her chin up so I could look into her eyes. "This is difficult. I want to be honest and open with you, so I must admit to my own disappointment. I also want you to be open and honest with me. Clearly, my feelings pale next to your own grief."

She pulled her chin away and looked down. "What woman doesn't want to give her husband sons? What woman fails to bear even one?"

I felt helpless. I wanted to console her, but I could not offer her any assurances—except my love and devotion. "Jathbiyya, I know this is hard. But know this—no matter what happens, I love you. I pledged my life to you, and I will keep that promise."

She looked back up at me with her tear-streaked face. "Truly? No matter what?"

I cradled her head in my hands, wiping the remaining tears off her face with my thumbs. "No matter what."

"Oh, Shah…I love you too." We embraced then, reveling in the consolation of peace and love found in each other's arms.

However, I had a duty as the sultan to care for my kingdom, and that duty overrode all else. "I have to make a trip, Jathbiyya."

She pulled back. "You do? Why?"

I hesitated. She was still raw from grief. But she was also a sultana. She should understand that the empire came first. "I must visit my brother and discuss the naming of an heir."

She stared back at me. Numb. No words.

"I must see to the empire. Not a week goes by without my viziers or the guards unearthing plots against me, discovering assassination attempts. I have many enemies. Your own country will renege on the treaty if we do not produce an heir. I must assure the succession for the empire."

Something new arose in her face. Something I had never seen. A glint in her eye, a tightening of her mouth. "Of course. You must take care of your empire. My feelings are of no import."

Did she not understand this? "Jathbiyya, I didn't say that. You are a ruler, too, in command of the household. Surely, you understand how important this is."

No response.

"I am not trying to hurt you—I'm trying to make sure we have the best life possible together." Not for the first time, I cursed the horrid luck that had placed me here, in this place, with these duties. She felt the sting of this wound, and here I was, forced to rub salt in it. I'd never hated my duty more than at this moment.

She whirled away from me and stood in anger. "The instant you declare another heir, you void the treaty with my father. He will surely declare war for the insult to me." She turned to face me. "If you would consider options before deciding on the most noble and therefore most inconvenient choice of action—"

"Inconvenient? How is honesty inconvenient?"

"You try to be honest, but everyone else is a liar, Shahryar. If you really want what is best for your kingdom, learn to lie. Learn to deceive."

Her admonition angered me. "All right, let's say you're right. Let's say that everyone is expecting deception. Let's even say that deception could be the best solution. What exactly do you suggest—that we fabricate a pregnancy and an heir for you to pretend to give birth to?" I crossed my arms.

"Exactly."

"Jath, I can't do that." She was being ridiculous, unreasonable. There was no way we could cover that up. Servants would talk, guards would gossip.

"No, you won't do that."

I stood up, towering over her. "Jathbiyya, it would never work. There is no way to keep a secret like that. And even if we did attempt to, it might be discovered years later—and then where would we be?"

She pressed her lips together. "We could do it. You just don't want to."

Damn her. "I want what is best for my people, my kingdom."

"And I am the one who will pay the price of that." She stalked out of the gardens.

I sat down, exhausted. We had experienced disagreements but had never fought like that before. *It's just her grief. She loves you; she loves that you are honest. Once she calms down, she'll see that this is the best way.* I kept trying to reassure myself, but it did not help.

That night, she was not waiting for me in my chambers, and I did not send for her. It was our first night apart since we had married. Despite my hope, I had a feeling that things had changed between us permanently.

Chapter 14
Day 733: Sulaila

Over two years had passed since wedding the sultan. Despite my logical reasoning, I had hoped that Shahryar would do something to acknowledge the day. However, he did not act as though anything was different, anything had changed. We woke, as usual, with prayers and breakfast before he left me to my own devices while he handled affairs of state. Ever since his confession in the gardens, we'd grown apart. I appreciated that fledgling trust he had given me, but it wasn't enough. Even the Pātakhti, with the success and unity we shared there, hadn't saved that trust. Nothing would be enough until I knew what had driven him to kill innocent women—and would eventually drive him to kill me.

I had reacted with sympathy and pity—a mistake, that. He left, cold rage burning the hands I placed on his arm in comfort. In my desire to grow closer to him, I had forgotten his pride. And now I didn't know how to come back to the sense of friendship we had planted earlier.

Oh, he still looked forward to our storytime each night. And I still had many tales to wile away—at least enough to occupy a year in the telling. Our breakfasts together were naught but stilted, polite conversation. And the rest of the days...

Shahryar had firmly restricted my freedoms. I only ever saw his chamber, the prayer room, the gardens, and my chambers. No more outings to the House of Wisdom, and I was to never venture out of the allowable areas. Part of me wanted to ask him for another trip out, but I was afraid. Afraid that he would use the opportunity to hurt me as I had unwittingly hurt him. Grinding my teeth in frustration, I walked out of the garden, but when I reached the corridor, I hesitated. Right would take me to my room. The safe option, no doubt. Going straight led to the main hallways, where the audience chamber and large dining hall were. Dangerous, because my presence would be seen and remarked upon. To the left, however, was a mystery.

Since Shahryar had failed to give his usual command for me to await him in my chamber, I decided to solve that particular mystery. I strode confidently down the hall to my right.

A pair of guards trotted after me: Mirko and a new one, whom I did not recognize. "Excuse me, my lady?"

I stopped.

The guards bowed, and Mirko continued, "Don't you wish to return to your room? His Majesty will expect you there this afternoon when he finishes his audiences."

I studied the man. He was sweating and not from the heat of the day. He shifted his weight from foot to foot, hands clenching and unclenching the spear he carried. I understood his predicament. If I was not where Shahryar expected me, the guard would be punished. And since I knew firsthand his merciless methods, I knew Shahryar would not hesitate to kill these two men for my transgression.

"Tell me, guardsman—did my husband command you to follow my orders?" I held his gaze in my unflinching one.

He winced. "I beg your pardon, my lady—I don't understand the question."

"Did the sultan ever, in any way, set an expectation that, while attending me, you were to follow my orders?"

Mirko tilted his head and brought his free hand up to rub the back of his neck. "Well, my lady, he did say we were to attend you. And he did tell us to make sure your needs were seen to..." He lifted both shoulders in an apologetic shrug. "I'm not sure if that answers your question, my lady."

I smiled. "Well, Guardsman Mirko, I need an adventure—alone. So I need to dismiss you."

Mirko sighed. "My lady, we are charged with your protection. We can't protect you if we aren't there." The shorter guard next to him nodded emphatically.

I smiled at both men. "Then Shahryar will have the dilemma of giving conflicting orders to deal with, won't he? That will keep him much too busy to mete out punishment to both of you."

The short guard started laughing aloud at this. It took Mirko another minute to understand, but once he did, a grin cracked his face. "My lady, I hope you will give us a full report after you discuss this with him." Both guards saluted, and marched off, shoulders still shaking with suppressed laughter.

I watched them leave, temporarily elated. But now it was time to enjoy freedom—my first freedom since my wedding two years ago. I walked down the corridor.

At first, it was fairly uneventful. The hall looked the same as the one by my room and by Shahryar's chambers. There were occasional doors, but since none of them were open, I decided against exploring there. The palace could host many sheikhs and their attendants, and I did not want to trespass on another's privacy. Finally, the corridor ended, splitting off to the right and the left with no option to continue forward. To the left, there was nothing to see. To the right, I heard faint laughter and conversation. I turned and followed my ears.

"He said—"

"No!"

"And then..."

A chorus of laughter erupted. I looked to my right at the enormous double doors, my curiosity piqued. I reached out a hand, then hesitated. Who knew what would lie beyond? As the gossiping picked up again, my fears were belayed. I grasped the handle and pulled the door open.

Silence. A full dozen women, clad in swathes of sheer silks, sat about on brightly colored cushions. They wore no veil, their hair tumbling about their faces like wild rivers through a mountain. All of them had turned to stare at me. I looked around but could see no one else.

"Excuse me, I must have, um, lost my way." I turned to leave.

"Wait!" one voice hailed me.

I paused, then looked over my shoulder.

This woman was older, strands of gray threading through her dark hair. She was tall, taller than me, but with an unmistakable strong jawline. "You are my son's wife." It sounded more like an accusation than a statement.

I nodded, afraid to speak.

"Please sit with us. I would share the noon meal with you." Her tone made it a command, not a request.

Still silent, I followed her further into the room and arranged myself on an available cushion. The other women watched me, some with interest, others with disdain, and still one or two with open animosity.

"How did you get past the guards?" asked one of the younger girls, who bit her lip immediately after asking.

"I did not see any guards." Should I introduce myself? They all seemed to know who I was—small wonder, since technically I should have been mistress of this entire palace.

As I considered what to do, the older woman knelt next to me, handing me a cup of coffee. "Remember, the sheikhs Jahan, Parham, Shadan, and Bijan are visiting. The guards are always lax when they're in town."

The other women giggled in response to the bold woman's assertion.

"Please forgive our forwardness. Here in the seraglio, we do not adhere to traditional feminine rules." Shahryar's mother turned one icy eye to the girl who had spoken up. "We thank you for coming to attend us—not many wives would."

Her words confirmed my suspicions. I had somehow stumbled upon the royal harem. No wonder Shahryar felt no need to be intimate with me. He had plenty of other options to pursue. It was almost a relief, especially since our relationship was so strained. Almost, because some small part of me was jealous. Except for a few chaste kisses on my forehead, he'd shown no physical affection toward me. And even those signs of care had gone away after his disastrous confession.

I dreaded each of our nights, knowing that while he enjoyed the stories, there was always the possibility that he would tire of me, with all the consequences that went along with it. These women could never understand—and why did I stay here? Shahryar would be furious if he found out.

One of the other girls leaned forward. "You have to tell us your secret!"

I paused while sipping the coffee. "What secret?"

"How you keep him with you every night!" Another girl scooted her cushion closer. "What is your trick? If I could do that, I could get out and marry a good man, maybe even a sheikh!"

The unequivocal admiration in her voice disarmed me. I had never had the opportunity to speak so with other women. Most of my companions in scholarship were men—few women sought out the House of Wisdom, much less went there regularly for research and learning.

The older woman smiled again. "Here, we are also encouraged to educate ourselves. Thus, we are more...outspoken than many other women."

Could I find freedom here? With these women, who, like me, longed for outside but were imprisoned inside?

"I—you flatter me. I have no great secret, other than knowledge, which is not a secret at all, but rather evidence of hard work and study." I sipped the coffee. Eyes were riveted on me. "I—"

"You have wrought wonders in Shahryar, dear. He still comes by to visit me, but believe me when I tell you he has eyes only for you."

I coughed, choking on half-swallowed coffee. "Eyes for me? My lady, he has not ever touched me, except to demonstrate control and power over me. I was relieved to find that this place, this opportunity existed—"

She reached out and placed a hand on my mouth, not in a masterful and commanding way, as Shahryar would have, but in a gentle correcting way, much like a mother with a child who needed to listen in order to learn.

"First of all, you are the lady of the palace, not me. You should address me appropriately. My name is Khaizuran." She removed the hand from my lips. "When wives learn of us, what we are, what we do, and what we gain from it, they tend to respond...negatively." She hesitated, then continued on, "If you like, I can call upon you from time to time. I would like to get to know you better, as you are, in many ways, a new-come daughter to me."

I looked into her eyes, which were the same rich brown as the coffee in my cup. Eyes that were alike, and at the same time different, from Shahryar's. Could I trust her? I had wanted an adventure and, apparently, gotten more than my fair share. Not trusting myself to speak, I nodded, curving my lips in the barest of smiles.

She smiled back. "Good. Thank you for taking some time for us. However, you should return to your chambers before you are missed."

I handed her my cup and rose, acknowledging the curtsies given by the other women before turning to leave.

"And Sutaita—" I turned to see Khaizuran had approached to escort me out. "Happy belated anniversary, dear."

My thoughts were in a jumble as I made the return journey to my own chamber. My studies had revealed many follies of humans to me, the keeping of concubines being one of them. Despite turning to the Prophet, the cultural tradition of a harem persisted. I wasn't ignorant of what the women were, but I had never expected to encounter them directly. Which seemed silly, especially since it was common knowledge that Shahryar was born of a concubine—of Khaizuran.

All that had happened in that room astonished me. It was well known that becoming a concubine could gain great political influence for a family.

Many girls sought that avenue for advancement, especially if an advantageous marriage was not possible. And now—I had met Shahryar's mother! Had any of his other wives had had the privilege?

In my thoughts, I had again lost awareness of the world around me. I barreled straight into Shahryar.

"Sutaita? What are you doing here?" He grabbed my shoulders to steady me, as the collision nearly toppled me.

I also grabbed his arms for stability. Looking up, I saw the thunderous expression on his face and inwardly cringed. "I...that is, I..." I took a deep breath. *Enough of this.* I looked him square in the eye, banishing any trace of fear from my mind. "I went to visit your mother."

His face stilled. His eyes moved slightly as he thought over all the meanings of what I had just told him.

We were both standing there, silently staring each other down, when Dunyazade appeared. "Sutaita! There you are! Where have you been all morning?"

Shahryar's mouth tightened. I sensed that Duny's appearance had forestalled a classic display of temper on his part.

Since he still seemed unable to formulate a sentence, I answered Duny curtly, "I met the sultan's mother."

"Oh!" Duny clapped her hands to her cheeks. "Oh Sutai, that's wonderful!" She turned to Shahryar. "You know, our mother died when we were both so young—thank you for introducing her to yours! How kind of you to understand how much a married woman would need someone to advise her!"

An awkward silence filled the hall. Shahryar turned, his malevolent eyes homing in on the two guards who inauspiciously chose that moment to reappear.

"Do not seek to reprimand them!" I ordered.

Shahryar turned back to face me, rage burning under the cool demeanor he wore like a mask. In an icy voice, he uttered two barely audible words. "Excuse me?"

I raised my chin. "You ordered the guards to obey me, did you not?"

His mouth opened and closed several times before he managed to get a word out. "You need guards. You do not know—you can't even imagine—the dangers here for you."

"And yet, somehow, I survived." My eyes narrowed. "I ordered the guards away. Promise me that you will not hold them accountable."

"I will do no such thing," he sneered.

"Very well. Please, show yourself to be capricious and indeterminate. Dunyazade and I could use the entertainment." I crossed my arms, knowing then that I had won. He would not want to look the fool in front of the guards and needed all the guards to feel confident in their duties. He couldn't take his anger out on them now that I had provoked him so thoroughly.

His face purpled with anger. "You will regret this." He pivoted and stalked off down the hall.

Duny whirled around to face me. "Sutaita! You are playing with fire!"

I had turned to watch Shahryar disappear down the corridor. "I know," I murmured. "And I'm not afraid of being burned—it's the cold that scares me more." And the frigid tolerance of the past several months, but I didn't want to confide that to Dunyazade.

One Thousand and One Days

Chapter 15
Day 745: Shahryar

It had been almost two weeks since Sutaita had met Mother, and I still raged. How much longer could I deal with her willful behavior? And now, I had to speak with Mother, to determine just how thoroughly Sutaita had compromised herself. *She should already know of any physical encounters spoken of in the seraglio—she's your wife!* I ignored that thought. I always ignored that thought and the temptation to kiss her full mouth, returning physically the passion she gave in her storytelling. It was my greatest regret and my greatest fear: that physical intimacy would destroy Sutaita, destroy what made her different from all the others.

I'd put off the visit for long enough. Dealing with Mother was always unsettling. She could always see the truths I fought to conceal and refused to tolerate what she termed my tantrum. I could remember that conversation like it was yesterday...

I had made up my mind. Ja'far tried desperately to get me to reconsider, but for the first and only time, I dismissed him from my presence. I summoned him again only to instruct him on the requirements for finding a new bride each night. When he tried again to dissuade me, I summoned a herald and dispatched him with the information about the law. Now it would be too late to change anything.

If I rescinded the law so soon after the herald announced it, I would look weak. It was always better to seem crazy than weak.

"Now, go find my wife for tonight." I left Ja'far standing there, staring at the floor, eyes glistening.

I had barely walked ten steps before a eunuch approached me. "Your Majesty, your mother requests your presence."

"Tell her I am busy." I kept on walking.

A eunuch guard appeared every day for a month. By then, I had married and executed thirty of the traitorous bitches. Every time, I sent the seraglio guards away until, one day, the captain of my own personal guard came. "Your Majesty, your mother demands you attend her immediately."

My lip curled in a snarl. "Demands? Immediately? Who does she think she is?"

The guard shifted from foot to foot. "She said you would say that. She told me to remind you that she suffered the pains of pregnancy and labor for you, and as such, you can never refuse her anything. She also bid me remind you of her service to you, both personally and royally."

Stymied, as usual. She was the only woman I knew whom I could not get the upper hand with. "Fine. Lead the way."

"Yes, Majesty." The guard gulped as he walked past me.

"Stop fretting."

"Of course, Majesty."

When I entered the seraglio, none of the girls gathered to greet me. *She must have sent them away*, I thought coldly. I didn't care. I stalked through the main room and toward my mother's suite. Slamming open the door, I looked about.

She was sitting calmly on a cushion, reading a book. The noise hadn't even startled her. I glared at her, then sauntered into the room and flopped down on a cushion. She turned the page, her eyes not even peeking up to acknowledge me. I hated how easily she could predict me.

I waited one minute, two, then five. She continued to read, the only sound the rustle of a page as it turned.

Finally, I slammed a fist down on the table. "What do you want, woman?"

Her eyes slowly rose to meet mine. She moved as if underwater, taking three times longer than needed to close her book, place it on another small table, and rearrange her skirts.

I stood and cursed, then glared at her. She stared back, not even blinking an eye. Finally, I turned and stalked back to my cushion and sat.

"What am I, Shahryar?" Her clear voice filled the room, filled my head, pushing everything else aside.

I crossed my arms and looked away. I would not answer her. I was the sultan and answered to no one.

She asked again, "What am I, Shahryar?"

I sneered at her. I would not be baited. I would win this confrontation and put her in her place.

After another long moment, she repeated herself again. "What am I, Shahryar?"

My internal temperature plunged. The delicious cold that sweetened my veins whenever I witnessed a wife's execution bubbled through me. I smiled. "You are a woman."

Of course, the soft, almost whispered voice did nothing to scare her. She merely nodded. "Yes. I am a woman. But what else?"

"What else matters?"

"Is that honestly all I am to you? Another woman?"

I scoffed. "Yes. That is all you are."

She nodded. "Then I will write the girls in the summer palace and dismiss them. Since I am a woman, like all others, you can entertain yourself with me. It will save you money."

I recoiled from her in horror. "That—what you suggest—Mother, that's blasphemous!"

"But all I am is a woman! If what you say is true, if that is all that matters, then nothing else about me should prevent that." She moved to begin disrobing herself.

"No! Please, no—Mother, don't!"

She looked at me and paused. "Then answer the question, Shahryar. What am I? All of it."

I swallowed. "You...you are a woman."

"Yes, we established that. What else?"

"You—you are a mother." I licked my lips, trying to think. "An advocate—if not for your support, I would not have won the throne."

"And what else?"

I thought and thought. "You—you are a concubine."

"A whore. Get it right."

I looked away from her.

"I am a whore. I lived in this palace at your father's largess, for the sole purpose of entertaining him. I bore him his first son, helped him navigate political quagmires, did everything a wife does, but without the title. I traded that option for a life of luxury. I made sacrifices for my future for him because I loved him.

"You, Shahryar, infuriate me. You had to endure my legacy, had to prove yourself worthy for the throne you now hold. I am so much more to blame for your life than those innocent girls you slaughter day by day. Why not kill me? I am no paragon of virtue. I am far from sinless. I have done shameful, base things. I have participated in events that would make you blush. I am all of those things in addition to being your loving and devoted mother. So why not kill me?"

I looked at her—really looked at her, for probably the first time in my life. She was right—everyone has duality, has good and bad things. And as I looked at her, I hated her for that. I could not have even one person in my life who was just good. Who would be honest and true. Who would never scheme and plot to take advantage of me.

I hardened myself. "Mother, all you do is prove my feelings right. If everyone is both good and bad, it is better that I enjoy the fresh good before bad spoils the budding flower." I stood to leave.

"As long as you have that edict in place, I will do nothing for you. You disgrace me, and you disgrace your father when you commit this atrocity of plundering your kingdom of women."

"So be it." I strode out of the room.

And now I stood outside the doors of the seraglio again. I threw open the double doors. Immediately, several of the girls there batted eyelashes and approached me, inquiring about my health, my day, and every other topic under the sun. I grunted in response until even the most persistent gave up.

Mother looked up when I burst into her private rooms. Her smile infuriated me.

"Why did you let her in here?"

"Please, Shahryar. Sit down. Would you like some coffee?"

"I would like to know why my wife was in the seraglio." I crossed my arms.

Khaizuran sighed. "Very well. I don't know why—I imagine she was bored."

"Bored. *Bored.*" I began pacing the room. "What is her problem? She has everything she needs."

"Does she now, Son?" Khaizuran's eyes peeked over the brim of her coffee cup. "And how long have you been married?"

I stopped short. How long had it been? *Oh, no.* It had been two years as of a fortnight ago. Two whole years given over to listening to her prattle on each night. But her stories were so intoxicating—the high point of my day.

"Are you so certain," Khaizuran continued, "that you are providing your wife with everything she needs?"

"Sutaita has no interest in a family or children. And I—" I blew out a breath instead of finishing. I couldn't tell my mother how I was afraid to express intimacy with Sutaita, that I feared she might change, become how all the others had been—lying and deceitful.

I glanced over at my mother. She sipped her coffee nonchalantly, as though oblivious to my inner torture. Unlikely—she noticed everything.

"I have deemed it best to wait. She is young."

"She is no younger than some of the other girls you happily bedded only to do away with them the next day. May I remind you, her continued life is the only reason I tolerate your presence here." Khaizuran rose and strode over to the door. "Young or not, consummated or not, your bride should have celebrated an anniversary with you—not been left to her own devices all day. I understand why both of you weren't ready to celebrate after only one year. But she is far too clever and active to remain in a cage, no matter how gilded." She leaned back on the door frame and crossed her arms. "I suggest you spend time with her instead of with your harem." She opened the door and raised an eyebrow. "Unless you want to entertain yourself here since you cannot bring yourself to fulfillment with your wife?"

A blush stained my cheeks. I left rather than answer that. I didn't need to look behind me to see my mother's smug expression as I departed. At times, I detested how accurately she could read people. At least, when I wasn't taking advantage of it.

But what could I do to mend things with Sutaita?

She deserves the truth.

That thought chilled me. But how could I demand honesty from her when I refused to give her my secrets? And last time I confided in her had destroyed the small beginnings we'd made. I started back toward the chambers and stopped. No. I couldn't do it. Couldn't face her pity, her compassion. Instead, I headed down the corridor to the court. I should govern instead of moping about with a woman.

As the day passed, however, I realized that I was wrong. Damn Mother for making me think—she always made me think. And I couldn't get that idea of duality out of my head. So Sutaita had not reacted as I wanted her to—that wasn't her fault. And I owed it to her to explain that. I would have explained it to Jathbiyya. Why would I not treat Sutaita with the same consideration?

That was the crux. All this time, I'd expected, demanded perfection from Sutaita, who'd never been married, never even considered that sort of relationship, and had no living mother to prepare her for it. And had paired those demands with mistrust and anger. What if her snooping had been to learn enough to be a good wife, to, as she'd said to me on that horrid day, learn from another's mistakes to avoid death? I owed her the whole truth.

I entered the chamber where Sutaita and Dunyazade both reclined on cushions, waiting for me. I looked at Sutaita—really looked at her. A shadow hung about her face, and the greeting she gave me never reached her eyes. My pain and fear were changing her. I'd never even thought about the damage the stress of coping with me and my insecurities was doing to her. And she'd never deserved any of it.

"Dunyazade, I wish to speak with Sutaita. There will be no stories tonight. Mirko will escort you home."

The guard stepped forward and gestured. Dunyazade and Sutaita exchanged a look before Dunyazade bowed and followed Mirko out.

Sweat beaded my forehead. I knew I had to do this, but it was hard—so hard. If I told her, explained everything, and she pitied me, I would have to send her away. I couldn't bear the pity. Not when I wanted something else, something more. That damn "more" she'd talked of when we first married, when she'd astounded the entire court reciting a parable like the most learned scholar.

I swallowed and jumped right in. No use putting it off. "Sutaita, I told you about my previous wife several months ago. I want to finish that story with you. But please, do not do as you did before and show me compassion. It—" I broke off, unable to explain.

"I understand, my lord. You are not one to desire fawning platitudes or emotional expression. I myself prefer the same. I'm just used to Father and Dunyazade…" Her voice trailed off, and a blush colored Sutaita's cheeks. "Please forgive my indiscretion then."

Instead of responding, I sat and continued my story.

After learning of my wife's barrenness, I set off to the family seat to see my brother. Things between Muhammad and myself had never been addressed, not truly. My bodyguard fidgeted beside me. Glancing at him, I noted the tightness of his shoulders, the whitening of his knuckles as his hands gripped his knees. He had counseled me against this visit, warned that it was merely a ploy to assassinate me and assume the throne.

Footsteps and the creaking of the door drew my attention away.

"Brother!" Muhammad smiled broadly, arms outstretched as he walked toward me.

My shoulders relaxed. He was happy to see me. We had worked it out. "Muhammad. It is so good to see you." I returned his hug warmly. As we pulled apart, I searched his eyes. He seemed genuinely pleased to see me. "How fare the Western provinces?"

Muhammad laughed. "Already politicking, Brother? This is unseemly. You have just arrived! Please, join me for some refreshments."

I smiled and followed him into the main hall. My stomach returned to its nervous tremoring. Muhammad not interested in politics—it seemed unnatural. But we had to make this work. I couldn't help wondering at the change in him, however.

As I entered a room tastefully decorated and well furnished with soft cushions and pillows, I understood the nature of his change. His new wife lay reclined in the corner. The sheer veil drawn over her face only drew attention to her bewitching visage. Full lips twisted up into a smile as she saw Muhammad approach. Sensuously, she arose and greeted him. He returned her greeting, and the heat between them...if I had half that passion in my marriage, I would be a lucky man. Her eyes alit on mine and seemed to smile at me while hinting at a secret.

Muhammad cleared his throat. "Shahryar, this is my wife, Sevilen."

"I am honored to meet you." I bowed slightly.

She smiled at me, bowing her head in return. "Please, let me serve you some refreshments. You have journeyed long." Her voice was deep and throaty yet still sweet. She gracefully resumed her position amidst the cushions and began portioning sweets and nuts onto plates.

Muhammad gestured, and I gratefully sat down as well, tired from several days' hard travel. I tasted the honey cakes and almonds and listened as Muhammad spoke at length about his governing successes.

It seemed that marriage had soothed him, calmed the temper from before. Instead of an iron fist, he heard petitions and sought to spread peace and unity instead of discord. I smiled, and he caught my eye, acknowledging the unspoken approval. He flushed slightly, ducking his head and shrugging.

"I am proud of you, Muhammad. You govern well. It seems that this life agrees with you—and that makes me glad. I desire only your happiness."

Muhammad glanced at Sevilen and smiled. Her eyes, kept demurely downcast, did not even notice him. "I have great reason to be happy, Brother."

We spoke for several hours further, long into the night. Sevilen had excused herself and departed hours ago. I did not want the day to end. I finally had him back—my brother, my family.

We finally embraced each other, yawning, before departing to our separate rooms. For the first time in over three years, I slept well.

I arose early in the morning, as was my custom. My excitement and happiness far outweighed the exhaustion of a late night. As soon as I had finished my morning prayers, I summoned my steward. I could secure the happiness. I could finally put all of the past behind us.

I had a new steward, recommended by my father's old vizier. A man named Abu Ja'far, married, with two young daughters. I liked his loyalty, prizing it above all else. He had worked hard with Tahmores to earn that trust.

The man came bustling in, prepared with paper and ink to take notes. I believe that he, like myself, was an early riser, for no hint of tiredness shadowed his face.

I greeted him with a smile and began without preamble to explain my plan. "Ja'far, I am so happy to see my brother—and to put the terrible past behind us."

Ja'far nodded and started to speak, but then hesitated.

Curious. We had developed a rapport, and he rarely held back his opinion from me. I turned to face him. "Ja'far, what is it? You are normally very forthwith."

Again, he hesitated.

I felt my stomach tighten. What could he possibly hesitate to say to me? "Ja'far, please. For the love of Allah, out with it. You have never been reticent before—what troubles you?"

Swallowing, Ja'far met my eyes squarely. "It is your brother's wife, Majesty. She approached me last night...in an inappropriate manner. I was afraid to say anything, even to you, since she seems to be the source of your brother's happiness—and our peace."

Silence filled the room. I just stared at Ja'far. My mind raced, but I could think of nothing to say. My poor brother! He would be heartbroken. More than heartbroken—I saw clearly last night that Sevilen meant everything to him.

No matter what happened, I could not win. I found a chair and collapsed into it. I just stared at the ground, trying desperately to find a solution—and failing.

Ja'far walked over to me, laying a comforting hand on my shoulder. We had spoken at length of my sadness for the rift between myself and my brother. He knew the extent of my grief. He knew how trapped I felt.

"Ja'far...please..." I managed to force the words out, though they felt like lead in my throat. "Advise me. Tahmores is not here...and I need it...please."

Ja'far hesitated again. He frequently offered advice, but while Tahmores was present, so that my official advisor could weigh in on the opinion. "Majesty, if I could offer a sound resolution, I would. However, the situation does not have any good answers."

I looked out the window at the open horizon bleakly. "Nothing?"

"Well, maybe if we discuss all the possibilities..."

"Fine. Do it."

Another moment of silence. Ja'far retrieved his writing materials and began taking notes. "Majesty, the main concern is whether we report this or not. If we report it, we risk earning the perpetual enmity of your brother. He may blame me, and through me, you, for his wife's dereliction. It could renew and cement the animosity between you. According to the law, she would have to be killed if it were revealed publicly. If we reveal it privately, however, your brother would still know the shame of an unfaithful wife. Your relationship would never recover fully."

I nodded. "So if we must report it, do so privately and let him decide...and prepare for the worst. But what if we don't? What if we keep it secret?"

Ja'far seemed to consider. He tapped his chin thoughtfully. "That is possible. But how much do you trust your brother's newfound welcome?"

I glanced at Ja'far sharply. "What do you mean?"

Ja'far took a deep breath. "It is possible, Majesty, that this is a test."

A frisson of fear shot through me. "A test? Of what?"

"Of you, Majesty." Ja'far stood and crossed back to me. "He may have instructed Sevilen to act this way, to test your loyalty. Remember, in his eyes, you stole a kingdom from him. He may be waiting to see if you are honest and respectful of what is his."

The enormity of the situation fully hit me then. No matter what I decided, there was risk—not just of my relationship with my brother, but of full-fledged civil war. The very thing I had worked so hard to avoid.

"I will cede the empire to him."

"Pardon?" Ja'far jerked up, stunned.

"It was always supposed to be his. I had planned to ask you to do that anyway. If I tell him but offer to step down, maybe it will placate him."

Ja'far frowned. "Majesty, you were named the heir. Stepping down now doesn't change that. It would still be almost impossible to prevent military action on your behalf."

I pushed down the ring of truth in his words. "Let me worry about that. Fighting is useless if the person you are fighting for disappears."

Ja'far waited another moment before bowing in acquiescence. "Of course, Majesty. Shall I arrange a meeting?"

"No." I stood and began walking toward the door. "We had plans to hunt together today. I will keep those plans, have one last day with my brother before I risk losing everything. And then I will tell him, make the offer."

It would solve all my problems. I could retire from rule with Jathbiyya, heirs be damned, and enjoy my life. I could save what was left of my family. It was my only option.

True to her word, Sutaita had schooled her face into an expressionless mask. A servant appeared, summoning us for dinner and interrupting my narrative. Sutaita followed my lead as I left the room and headed for the dining hall.

I didn't know whether to feel angry or relieved that she asked no questions, demanded no response. Apart from soft yet witty answers to my queries, she kept her thoughts and feelings to herself. As I had asked.

So why was I still unhappy?

Chapter 16

Day 801: Sulaita

It was my eight hundred and first morning with my husband. As usual, we broke our fast in the garden. Normally, he tried to guess at the ending of the story I was currently telling or trick me into revealing a plot twist or secret. It seemed a sort of game—him trying to convince or maneuver me into revealing more of a story, and me answering his questions without giving him the information he so desired.

I must confess, I enjoyed the battle of wits. It challenged me in a way no one else ever had. What had started as me doing everything within my power to obey him and respond without losing the power my stories held over him had turned into something far more intimate than I could have dreamed. We would both laugh at some of my more outrageous responses, and he took great delight in trying to trap me. He never succeeded, and lately, I wondered if that was for lack of trying as opposed to an inability to truly corner me.

It felt good to laugh with him. Some mornings, I could forget the cloud hanging over my head, the fate awaiting me that spun closer and closer.

As we finished eating, however, something was different. Shahryar seemed nervous. He had barely touched his breakfast—a departure from his norm. And the cloud of his first marriage still hung between us. As requested, I had not reacted emotionally to his story.

I also knew it was far from over. His brother was dead, not ruling the empire, and until I solved that mystery, I would be in danger. But for this morning, this day, I was safe.

As servants cleared our plates, his eyes met and held mine. For the first time ever, they seemed open and seeking instead of closed off. Before I could wonder at this subtle yet significant change, he stood and walked around the table to me. He pulled my chair back, turning it so I stared up at him.

Taking both my hands in his own, he kissed each one on the knuckles. The kiss was as soft as the white sands on an oasis. He had begun touching

113

me, little touches on my arms and face, but this was the first time he had ever placed his lips on my skin, instead of on my hair or veil. A slight tremor raced up my arm. My eyes widened.

"My dear Sutaita. I have a confession to make." He sighed heavily.

I waited patiently. I knew this man had demons—his hate and anger had to have come from somewhere. He had seemed to gentle over the past year, but there were still moments when fury blazed in his gaze.

"Sutaita, I have avoided treating you as a man should treat his wife. I have treated you as a prisoner, when you should be my valued confidante. I...I will start trying to be better."

It was all I could do to keep my jaw from crashing onto my lap. Where on earth had this statement come from? In all our time together, this man had never set pride aside and apologized. Goosebumps broke out over my skin. "If you think a kiss and sweet words will get me to tell you if the princesses help Hasan, you have not been paying attention the past eight hundred nights."

A smile lit his face and, for the first time I could recall, reached his eyes. He pulled me up by my hands and dropped one to reach a finger up to trace the outside of my face. Softly, ever so slowly, his hand reached around the back of my neck, cupping my head. He gently leaned down while pulling me toward him.

His lips touched mine. They were warm and tasted of the honey and wine from breakfast. My heart fluttered, not in fear as it had most of this past year, but with something else—something new. I felt a warm sensation in my stomach, like the uncurling of smoke in the air. These new sensations seemed to overwhelm me. I clung to him, afraid that I would fall.

His other hand had reached around my back, and he supported me. He drew back from me, ending the kiss. How long had it lasted? Had it been minutes? Or barely a second? My calm countenance was gone. Instead, my breath came heavy, and my whole face burned. I felt as though he had ripped off the mask of serenity I wore and saw the turbulent self underneath—the self that feared death at his hands, loved and feared for my sister, and the secret desire I had never spoken to anyone about.

Clearing his throat, he said hoarsely, "Until tonight, Sutaita."

I had asked my maid to send Dunyazade away. A cowardly choice, but I didn't want to face—no, couldn't face—my sister just now. As I paced about my chamber, my mind reviewed the encounter over and over again. I had tried to sit and study, but nervous energy filled me.

What had changed? And who could I talk to? For the first time in many years, I fervently wished my mother still lived, that I might ask her what to do. I had no experience with a man, knew not what Shahryar meant by that kiss. Did he know it would unsettle me so? Put me in a state and use that weakness against me? *But, lately, he's been more friendly and supportive than before.* I set my jaw, squashing such thoughts. He hadn't rescinded that edict. And as long as that remained, I was in danger.

With a sigh of frustration, I sat down at my study table again, determined to do something productive today. A sheet of parchment caught my eye. It was my list from months ago, trying to piece together the actions leading to a terrible edict that killed dozens of women. Well, no time like the present to revise it.

I frowned. The same explanations still worked. I knew there was conflict between Shahryar and Jathbiyya, knew that conflict somehow led to her death. I also knew that Shahryar meant to abdicate in favor of saving that marriage. Did Byzantium object? And declare war? Did Muhammad die in defense of the empire, or was he killed by a jealous and angry Jathbiyya? And what had happened to Sevilen?

Scowling, I tucked the parchment away again. I had more questions but no answers. The archives. I had promised Shahryar not to look at the personal family history, promised to ask instead. I ground my teeth in frustration. He would never tell me. He would give me the same cover-up—and I was certain by now that there was a cover-up—and move on with life.

A small laugh sprang to my lips. I was well and truly trapped. If I disobeyed and sought out the information on my own, Shahryar would surely kill me. But waiting for him to be honest was as useful as waiting for a new spring in the desert.

I gathered my things, determined to walk about the palace since that was the only outlet for my energy. Spying Mirko standing just outside my chamber, I paused.

A guard announcing the evening meal. I remembered telling Duny I knew where to start looking. Then a comment from one of the concubines came back to me: *"Remember, the sheikhs Jahan, Parham, Shadan, and Bijan are visiting. The guards are always lax when they're in town."*

Who would see everything, be part of any execution, and be trusted to keep the family's secrets? Guards. And why would they be lax when certain sheikhs visited? I walked back to my table and fetched the latest stack of paperwork for Manoush. It was time to visit the archives, and I could learn something about this mystery without breaking my promise to Shahryar.

Arash managed to keep his face straight as I brought in Manoush's work. Based on his continued chilly reception of me, I gathered that he hated how I circumvented his attempts to keep me out of the archives. Luckily for me, the records for affluent sheikhs were not kept anywhere near the family records. It made sense, since those families also had access to the archives, at least to review their family history. But the archivists did not want these politically-powered families nosing through the royal family history. I kept one eye on my surroundings as I worked, copying Manoush's short notes into longer records for an archivist to file away—after Arash did his spying. When I was alone, I stopped and studied the shelves next to me, locating and removing the books I needed. Jahan, Parham, Shadan, and Bijan were all newer sheikhs, granted land near the sultan's family seat to the west. I slipped the books under my piles of paper in case a scribe passed by.

My heart was in my throat, I was so nervous. If I was right, and something was here, Arash would know in an instant. And he'd tell Shahryar. I focused on my copying, trying to bring calm and stillness to my body.

When a servant summoned Arash away, I took the opportunity to duck into one of the many copying chambers lining the walls of the archives. These little alcoves were built for silencing external noise and discouraging interruption. After all, it's difficult to interrupt someone you cannot find.

I opened the first book and couldn't believe what I read. Jahan had been granted land, making him a sheikh, on the same date as Muhammad's death. When all four books declared the same thing, I knew it could not be a coincidence. These four men, nobodies before, became sheikhs when Muhammad died. A note on one of the books caught my eye. Volume 39. Volume 39 of what? Following a hunch, I gathered all my things and left the alcove. I returned the books of the sheikhs' history to their shelf, trusting my confidence and regular work in the archives to prevent anyone from noticing that aught was amiss. I then went to the section that detailed the servants and workers in the palace. Trailing my hand down the spines, I selected volume 39 of the guard roster. Opening it, my stomach sank. Sure enough, Jahan, Parham, Shadan, and Bijan had all served as the sultan's personal guard—and before that, as Muhammad's.

One Thousand and One Days

Chapter 17
Day 861: Shahryar

Something had changed in Sutaita. I couldn't be sure what, but I knew something was different. I called myself ten kinds of fool for kissing her. The look of shock on her face said it all. Ever since that day, she'd been more reserved, if that was even possible. I had to find out why she was closing herself off.

"My dear Scheherazade, I find myself worried."

"Worried, my lord?" Her eyes widened slightly, but nothing else on her face gave away any emotion.

I tried to smile. "Yes. I feel as though you've been somewhat quiet for the last couple of months. Did I do something to upset you? Are you unhappy?" I tried to keep my real worry from my voice, that kissing her without asking, without making sure she was ready, had ruined any possibility of sharing real passion.

A shadow flitted across her features. Yes, she was distressed about something. But would she confide in me?

I saw her throat tighten. "My lord, I am apprehensive. I've asked you about your past many times. Mine is simple and open. You've known my father for many years, and court gossip about me was quite correct. I am a scholar, always haring off to the library to read and study. I'm one of very few female scholars who've sought recognition in study and attained it."

She looked up, and I swear, I felt her eyes bore into my very soul. "But you've given me small bits and half-truths. I've kept my promise to you and ceased researching the family in the archives. You told me to ask you my questions. I have, repeatedly. You don't answer them. You evade them or, when pressed, give just enough of a response to claim you've answered, when in reality, you've been more evasive than forthcoming." She took a breath, then continued, "In our time together, I've learned that trust is crucial. Trust is something that, for whatever reason, frightens you. And yet you cannot demonstrate for me the trust you want me to bestow upon you. No more lies. What happened with your brother and your first wife?"

Her jaw set, she continued to stare me down, yet I could see a small flicker of uncertainty in her eyes.

In that moment I wanted, more than anything, to tell her. Confide in her the whole truth, consequences be damned. But every time we took a step forward, something happened to pull us back. She spoke in court; then my anger pushed her away. She supported me, then went behind my back. I shared some stories, and she reacted with pity instead of acceptance.

And there was one other problem. Sutaita was smart—too smart. She wouldn't believe the official story, where the lies had gaps large enough to drive a herd of camels through them. She would question, and if she questioned the wrong people, my biggest and most dangerous secret could be unearthed. I couldn't let that happen.

I considered my options. And considered what would happen if she did seek this information on her own. She could easily ask the wrong person and end up in danger. My thoughts flitted back to our kiss. She'd felt warm and accepting, opening herself as a bud to the sun. It felt like euphoria. Could I live with myself if something I did put her in danger? And as I looked into her eyes, I realized one other thing: I couldn't keep lying to her.

Maybe just a little of the truth. Just enough to sate her, as I'd been doing. Enough to steer her toward the official lie and have her stop asking questions. I cleared my throat. "You recall that there were some problems with my first marriage?"

She nodded, mouth and jaw softening slightly, but refrained from speaking.

"Well, I had determined to handle the inheritance of the empire by abdicating in favor of my brother. After our hunt, I went to tell him immediately, in case he and Sevilen were testing me...

I went in search of him, sparing no time and hoping to avoid another misunderstanding. After all this time, after everything, how could he still doubt me?

I rushed through the palace, searching everywhere I could think of for my brother. After our hunting trip, we'd agreed to clean up and meet for refreshments, so I hoped to find him before he found Sevilen and invited her, before time stole my ability to rebuild that relationship.

I finally arrived at his personal chambers, having failed to find him in the gardens or the dining area. I heard noises and smiled. I knew now the reason for his delay. He must be with the lovely Sevilen. It had been a test after all. Thank Allah for her—his marriage to her had finally ended the feud between us.

She must have finally shown him the value of family. It warmed my heart to know of the deep and abiding love between them. I turned and left, creeping on my toes to avoid making noise and drawing attention to myself. I succeeded until I tripped and fell on my face, a loud oath roaring from my lips as I tumbled down.

The noises in the chamber stopped. In my clumsiness, I had disturbed them. Too late to preserve the feeling now. Standing and glancing around to see if anyone saw, I pulled my askew clothing into place. I strode into the chamber to see a strange man hastily clothing himself. Sevilen grabbed at the sheets and yanked them to her shoulders, glaring at me. The strange man, someone I did not recognize, turned and saw me. With a yelp, his eyes widened. He started, then grabbed one last article of clothing before rushing past me and down the hallway.

"Sevilen! What is the meaning of this?"

The woman's lips turned up into a smirk. "It is an affair. What does it look like, Shahryar?"

"How could you... Muhammad *loves* you, more than I have ever seen any man love a wo—"

"His pawing is barely tolerable. I put up with it for the added value: this palace, and the money and riches his title includes." She sneered, somehow managing to still look absolutely devastating. Dropping the sheet, she slunk out of bed, moving slowly and smoothly like a snake. "That man is nothing, just a distraction from the boredom of being here constantly."

My forehead broke out with sweat. Her naked body tantalized me, swaying as she moved closer to me. I tried to move, to leave, to turn away, anything. My body refused to move, as if it had changed into stone.

Her full, luscious lips curved in a smile, but her eyes glittered with a cold, cruel light. "See, you cannot help yourself. You desire this body. Every man desires this body. And since none of them truly care about me, I take care of myself first." She reached out and grabbed my cloak, forcing my head close to hers.

I swallowed, trying to force the lump out of my throat. "Sevilen, this is wrong. According to the Law, I should have you killed..."

She laughed. "And since your Law also doesn't care about me, I refuse to kneel to its demands." She kissed me then.

I finally was able to move. I brought my hands up to her shoulders and forcefully pushed her back...right as Muhammad stormed into the chamber.

Muhammad's eyes darted from me to Sevilen and back to me. His lips moved, but no words came out. His shoulders rose with each breath, the height increasing more and more until his hold body was shaking. Red-faced, he shoved a finger in my chest and finally managed to utter a single word: "*You!*"

"Muha—"

"*Out!*"

"Please, just let me—"

"*Leave! Now!*"

Fearing his growing rage, I left, hurrying down the hall and back to my chamber. Ja'far was there waiting for me. A small tightening of his lips was the only expression on his face.

I hung my head, ashamed. Every time I tried to repair the relationship with my brother, something happened. Something went wrong. "We must depart immediately."

Ja'far said nothing and swept out of the room to murmur instructions to the bodyguard. He returned and began packing his notes and scrolls with a studied economy of movement. I collapsed on a cushion. Part of me wanted to deny everything—pretend as though it never happened.

And Muhammad. How must I look to him, thief first of his kingdom, then of his wife? I realized there would be no mending of fences after this, no repairing the relationship.

If I came forward about witnessing Sevilen's adultery, at best she would be exonerated for lack of witnesses. At worst, she would be stoned, as well as the other man I saw. And if Muhammad could find two other men willing to witness that I had slept with Sevilen...my head would be on the chopping block. Why did he have to appear right then? A few minutes earlier or later, and there would have been no problem. It just didn't make sense.

A thought crossed my mind. Poking my head out, I gestured to the guard. He approached with a salute.

"Yes, my lord?"

"Send someone to Muhammad's chamber—quietly. Look for any places to listen or hide, spyholes, anything."

"Sir, Ja'far has already requested this."

I was astonished. I truly had a faithful servant in him. He could easily have looked after himself instead of investigating the situation for me.

"Very well. Return to your post, and thank you."

"Sir." The guard saluted again and returned to keeping watch down the hall.

Within an hour, Ja'far and a servant had packed everything, and we were collecting our mounts from the stable. "Your Majesty, there are ways to spy on the main chambers." Ja'far's shoulders lifted in a shrug. "I cannot prove that you were set up, but neither can I rule out the possibility."

"Then perhaps it is best that we are ready to depart."

I was about to mount up when Muhammad stormed out of the main palace, dragging Sevilen by the wrist. He looked around and, seeing me and my entourage in the stables, marched in our direction, still yanking Sevilen along after him. He threw her down to the ground in front of me. "Confess." His hard voice, clipped and terse, was directed at her instead of me.

She looked up from the ground, limbs sprawled from the fall. Tears streamed down her face, and the glorious mane of black hair was knotted and strewn about, plastered to her face where tears had moistened it. "My lord, please. I love you, please for—"

"*Confess!*"

Her whole body shook. I tried to catch my brother's eye, but the whole of his attention was on his wife.

Looking back down, I saw her bow her head, pink shame tinting her cheeks. "My—my lord...I must...must con-con-confess...I...I tried...to se-se-seduce you."

My heart stopped. I looked up at my brother, eyebrows raised.

"The slut told me after you left. I remand her to you for punishment. Should be several hundred lashes. Then please depart so I can deal with my shame."

I hesitated. He didn't know about what had happened before. I recalled what Ja'far had told me that morning. The woman was indeed unfaithful, and lashes were unlikely to change that.

Could I accept the peace offering and cuckold my brother? Allow another bastard, but this time one without royal blood, on the throne? Part of me wanted to do this, take the easy way out. But surely, above all others, I owed my brother honesty. Let him determine how to proceed. With just my word, we could not prove the adultery, so surely that was the best option—right?

"Brother, I must confess too...I saw something happen." I took a deep breath, then continued, "Your wife had a lover in her bed. It was after scaring him away that she turned her attentions to me."

Before my brother could do anything, Ja'far also approached. "My lord, if I might add, she also approached me and tried to seduce me. Shahryar was at your chambers because he sought you out to inform you of such."

It was like a dam had burst. Servants and attendants all rushed forward to share stories of Sevilen's innumerable attempts to seduce them, with even a few shamefacedly confessing to acquiescing. My brother just stood there. The planes of his face hardened into stone, and his entire countenance seemed as though his very humanity left him.

When the last confessor finished, he looked at me with blank eyes. "You know the law." With that, he turned and departed, trudging step by lonely step back to his palace.

For my brother's sake, I answered the demand of the law swiftly. Once he was back in the palace, I called for my sword. A guard took charge of Sevilen, who was still sobbing in disbelief. Many of the men stayed as witnesses of justice. I led the entourage out past the stableyard, found a decent rock, and bade Sevilen lay her head upon it.

She was forced to comply by the guard and fought him with all the ferocity she could muster, flailing and lashing out, biting, and clawing with her nails. In the end, however, he held her down.

I raised my saber high. "In the name of Allah, let justice be done." I swung down hard and severed her head from her body. Beheading is a bloody affair, and while many of the onlookers jeered and reveled in the gory mess, I left as soon as I had instructed the guard to ensure that no one desecrated the body.

After a thorough search, I finally found my brother hiding in a niche in his garden. The alcove lay behind several fronds of palm, and if not for the sound of his weeping, I would have overlooked him entirely.

I lifted the palm and cleared my throat.

Muhammad froze, looked to see who disturbed him, and immediately looked away. "Leave me alone," he rasped.

"Brother, I am so—"

He whirled back around. "I said, *leave me alone*! Haven't you done enough?"

"But Muh—"

"*Leave*! As soon as you are around, *everything* gets ruined!"

"I didn't do any—"

"I don't *care*!" He shot up off the bench he had been sitting on. "You were supposed to just be my half brother! You were supposed to just be my *friend*. But I guess that wasn't good enough for you."

"Muhammad, I never—"

"If you had just kept your mouth shut...I was willing to forgive and forget. Punish her and move on. But you had to shame me, lower me, in front of my entire household." His head hung down, his countenance defeated.

My heart sank. No matter what, I always managed to do the wrong thing with Muhammad. Now it seemed I could never fix this.

I tried to swallow the lump in my throat and failed. "I am so sor—"

His eyes flashed as he jerked his head up. I knew then that there was no repairing this. His rage was so far gone, he could no longer hear me. "Don't apologize to me. I don't want your pity," he sneered.

"Well then, what do you want?"

His eyes flashed as he looked up, glaring at me. "I want you to suffer as I have."

There was no answering such blatant anger and malice. I nodded my respects and left quietly. I gathered my entourage and departed for Baghdad moments later.

Sutaita didn't speak when I finished my story. She waited, trying to gauge my feelings.

I wished I could tell her how I felt. Even years later, there was so much hurt and shame wrapped into the saga with my brother that just thinking of it made me want to rage and cry at the same time. And I had been honest, just enough. The faithlessness of Sevilen set in place everything else that happened. As they always did whenever I recalled the entire sordid tale, my thoughts continued to my own betrayal, my own horror. I wished, more than anything, I could just make it stop.

Then why do you make yourself relive it each night? Why did you inflict that same torture on innocent women?

That damned conscience kept railing at me. And now, after all this time with Sutaita, the thought of killing her made my chest feel tight. While it wasn't the same sense of loss I'd felt when I'd learned of Jathbiyya's treachery, it was still something I recognized and hated: fear.

"So I assume from that story that Muhammad was unable to take over ruling the empire." Sutaita's warm, rich voice broke through my thoughts.

"No," I tried to say, but the words stuck in my throat. Clearing it, I tried again. "No, he did not. What he did was even worse, but..." I looked at her. Could I trust her with this secret? If she betrayed me, it would all be over. Everything would fall down around me.

No. I'd been married to Jathbiyya for years, and she'd still betrayed me, played me all along. I simply couldn't take that chance again.

"It reignited conflict with him. This fight made the previous succession conflict look like a squabble between Manoush and one of the kitchen maids."

Sutaita raised an eyebrow. "Have you seen those squabbles? They are no small thing, my lord."

I chuckled softly. Allah bless her for making this easy. *For making it easy to lie to her, when you would slaughter her should she dare do the same to you.*

I took a breath and tried to steady my voice. I'd done the first part, laid the foundation of truth. Now for the lie. "Anyway, he was killed by a Byzantine spy, which started the war with Byzantium. I lost them both and had to lead a divided nation into war."

Sutaita nodded at what I said and offered me a smile, but it did not reach her eyes.

My heart sank, and that strange piercing feeling returned. I'd come to think of it as guilt. *Damn it. She knows I'm lying!*

Chapter 18
Day 921: Sutaita

The past two months had been absolute torture.

I'd done my best to play the part—act the dutiful wife, and accept the blatant lie Shahryar told me. But I've never been good at dissembling. He knew I knew he was lying. It was like a complicated and intricate dance, where we were both so focused on not stepping on each other's toes that we had stopped seeing each other.

Was this what the rest of my life would be like?

It felt so hopeless. I had thought I was miserable before, but this was even worse. After sharing that kiss, I'd hoped, prayed, wished that it meant things were finally moving forward, that Shahryar would finally trust me, tell me the truth, and show me the path to heal his wounds and fight the demons that haunted him. For his story convinced me of one thing: Sevilen's duplicity was part of the ghost that haunted him.

I couldn't confide in Duny. This might be a test, a test of loyalty. And if Shahryar learned I had shared a secret with my sister, no story in the world could entice him to stay his hand. And the part where he'd been honest? That part was dangerous. It opened the way for questioning the public record of Muhammad's death. He was no victim of war, that was for certain. Shahryar's eyes had evaded mine when he told that part, and his neck flushed.

Confiding in my father was also out of the question. That story, more than any other, convinced me that my father was entirely devoted to the sultan. I recalled when I'd offered to marry Shahryar. Father had been devastated but had accepted out of duty to the sultan. He'd had the means to send both me and Dunyazade far away, make us impossible prospects. He hadn't done that.

Deep down, part of me had started wondering if he was complicit in all this. Surely, he knew the truth—him, Shahryar, and four guardsmen turned sheikhs. And yet Father didn't see fit to warn me, to explain the reality of my situation. Or, as I was beginning to understand, not only wouldn't warn me, but would drag me in front of my husband and demand my death himself if he learned I was seeking this information out.

I couldn't even ask Khaizuran. While she saw just about everything that happened at court and was a trove of wisdom in navigating court politics, this secret and cover-up was beyond the glittering backstabbing of the Baghdad elite.

With a scowl, I pulled out a page of successoral calculations and began work. Better to use my remaining time in scholarly pursuit than stewing in my own failure.

An hour or so later, I heard voices in the hall.

I recognized Dunyazade's laugh as she said, "I really like your story so far!"

"Well, I am not as adept a teller as Sutaita, but I guess I have had an interesting life." That was Shahryar's deep voice.

Seconds later, Shahryar and Dunyazade entered the room.

"My dear wife, I ran into your sister on her way in to see you and decided to escort her here." Shahryar clutched a piece of parchment and shifted his weight nervously from foot to foot.

Why was he nervous? "Thank you, my lord. Your continued attention to my family is estimable."

Duny looked from me to the sultan and back again. With a shrug, she selected a seat and plopped her stack of books on the table.

With a nod to both of us, Shahryar left.

"Sutai, are you all right? You've been somewhat broody for the past several weeks."

I shook my head. "It's nothing."

"You're clearly upset. You know you can talk to me. What is it?"

I took a deep breath and let it out slowly. "It's just this whole situation. I'm running out of stories, and we're no closer to finding a solution." *And now I'm well and truly stymied, with no way to learn the truth.* A tear slipped from my eye. "I don't know what he'll do." And I didn't. For the first time in over nine hundred days, I felt truly helpless.

Duny stood and walked over to drape her arms around me in a side hug. "Oh, Sutai. You've got nothing to worry about. Can't you see how much he loves you?"

I stiffened underneath her caring embrace. She didn't know—couldn't know. I tried to relax, to calm the taut muscles in my shoulders. "Of course. I guess you're right."

And now I was lying to my sister.

When had I changed from an honest, forthright person into someone who kept secrets and covered up other's faults? And how could I change back?

Later that night, I waited in Shahryar's chamber as usual. I did my best to keep my face smooth, betraying no hint of my inner turmoil.

Shahryar entered and paused when he saw me. His eyes looked me over, considering.

I bowed my head. *Please, please, don't be mad. Don't lash out at me.*

The first few months in our marriage had been trying. Shahryar reacted explosively to the slightest provocation. Combined with my constant state of fear—not too different from the terror I felt now—I'm honestly surprised that he had never struck me. He grabbed my wrist hard enough to bruise, yes, but never a deliberate slap or blow. And after that one time, when he saw the bruise, something changed. Or so I hoped.

Shahryar walked over to a nearby cushion and sank into it. "Did you wish to continue your story?"

My mouth dry, I answered, "Only if it pleases you, my lord."

Silence stretched between us.

"I would have your honesty, Sutaita. Why do you tell me stories?"

My hands shook. If I told him the truth, he would kill me for conspiring against him. If I lied, he would know and take that as proof that he was right to kill his wives, right to prevent being manipulated or deceived by women.

"Sutaita?" His voice was clear and demanding.

I shook my head.

"Why do you hesitate? Is it so hard to say?" he asked.

Miserable, I nodded.

"Look at me."

A direct command, one I dared not refuse. I lifted my chin, showing him eyes glittering with unshed tears.

A shadow crossed his face. He stood and walked to the window, slipping his hand into his pocket. He studied the view before turning to face me. "If you cannot answer my question, can you at least tell me why?"

I closed my eyes. "Because I am frightened, my lord."

"Frightened for yourself or of me?"

It took all my courage to answer him. "Of you, my lord," I whispered, looking up at him.

He turned back to the window and leaned against the sill. For several moments, we stayed there, afraid to speak, afraid that anything we said would ruin the infinitesimal shred of regard that remained between us.

Finally, he spoke. "In that case, I am happy to hear more about the merchant and the robbers, provided you wish to continue." He walked over to me, crouched down, and gently extended a hand to my chin. "But if you are not up to it, we can retire, and you can continue on another night."

The unspoken promise hung between us. He would not kill me outright. Should I risk it? Should I reveal everything to him, my fears and, even more, the tiny spark of hope still living after two and a half years of struggle?

Instead, I wiped my eyes, cleared my throat, and continued telling the story.

Chapter 19
Day 953: Shahryar

Sutaita's refusal to answer kept bothering me. I suspected the stories were a ruse, a means to an end. She'd played her game well. I'd been so engaged, so intrigued at the onset, that she'd slipped past my guard and wormed her way into my heart before I'd realized it.

I knew that staying alive herself was only part of it. Sutaita'd hoped to stay alive long enough for other girls to come of age so that her father wouldn't have to turn around and offer her sister to me. *To slaughter.*

In the past month, I'd gotten to know Dunyazade rather well. She and Sutaita were inseparable, spending hours with heads tilted against one another in studies. That in and of itself baffled the mind. None of the other women I'd ever known bothered with math and science. If I saw their heads together, it was usually when exchanging gossip.

But the sisters were happy to research, read others' work, and attempt to re-create it. I had a feeling that, if I let her, Sutaita would leave for the House of Wisdom each morning and return only as the sun sank below the riverbank.

One part of this was the niggling thought that kept coming back: that Sutaita had done this not out of love, but as part of a plot, part of a way to manipulate me. For as long as she lived, even at my behest, I broke my own law, and thus my rule was weakened for it. Had she manipulated me this entire time in some grand effort to seize power, to ruin my life? Or, even worse, through her stories change me, alter me into someone who would not only stay his hand from executing her, but into someone who would change, find happiness in love and marriage and the unique companionship we shared.

As I considered it over the next several days, it seemed silly. No one in their right mind would try to change someone by telling stories.

But what if stories really were that powerful? I had stayed my hand for over two years now, waiting to reach the end of one story. But that ending had to wait for three other stories, and once told, another story began.

What if, through the simple act of spinning tales, my wife had actually changed me?

And, even more worrisome, what if I was less—less of a man, less of a ruler—because of that change?

And at the same time, I had loved the time with Sutaita. What had started as a mere fascination had changed into something else, something more. That "more" Sutaita had spoken of that one day in my court. It was that day I realized how much I desired a true marriage, how much I wanted that companionship, that closeness.

I was sitting in my private office, reviewing correspondence. I opened a plain envelope, the next on my stack. The letter was brief and to the point.

> Each day you do not kill her, you defy your own law.
> If the truth comes out about this edict, we are all at risk.
> Kill her yourself—or else we will.

And the four guards I'd raised to power had each signed it.

"Ja'far!" My voice was so loud, the door to the office rattled.

The vizier rushed in. "Yes, my lord?"

Without a word, I thrust the parchment at him. His swarthy face paled as he read it.

"What should I do?"

Ja'far shook his head, eyes wide with horror. "I do not know, my lord."

I slammed my hands on the table. "That's not good enough! You're my vizier, my most trusted advisor. Advise me!" My anger barely masked the panic coursing through me. I had to fix this, had to figure this out. The thought of anything happening to Sutaita... I swallowed, fighting the gorge rising in my throat.

Unasked, Ja'far sank into a nearby chair. "I don't know that there's anything you can do. Even if you reverse the edict, you did break your own laws. If someone were to bring you to court, you would have to supply evidence, and the truth of your brother and first wife would have to be disclosed."

Tapping the parchment, Ja'far continued, "We have to find out what they really want: if they are merely concerned for the cover-up or if they know something else. Or—" and he hesitated at this "—if they've betrayed you, and someone else pulls their strings."

The walls felt as if they were closing in on me. I blew out a sigh. "What a mess. Well, I can send someone I trust to find out what their intentions are."

Ja'far slumped, a surprising action of the usually comported man. "It would have to be me, Your Majesty. We can't send someone who doesn't know the whole truth already. If they're worried about losing their status, we can't bring a newcomer into the fold."

I studied my chief vizier, and then I understood the haunted expression in his eyes. As long as that edict remained, Ja'far lived every day in fear of losing his eldest daughter. And while a few maidens within the city had come of age in the past year, it would be only days after Sutaita died before Dunyazade would, theoretically, be the next victim. And still, the man had remained loyal to me. *What had I ever done to deserve such devotion?* Guilt wrapped around my other intense emotions. I'd shut them out for so long, having this many swarm around me made it difficult to breathe, let alone process everything happening.

After taking a moment to settle myself, I crossed the room and opened the door. "Go to Mirko and tell him, on my orders, to keep the sultana in sight at all times. No exceptions."

The guard outside the office saluted me and took off down the hall.

I closed the door. "I wish I knew what to do, my friend."

Ja'far's mouth tightened, and his eyes flashed in anger. He launched to his feet. "Reverse your damned edict already!"

"You know I can't do that!"

"In Allah's name, why not?"

We glared at each other. "She's a mere woman. I can't trust her. She could betray me at any time." The lie fell so easily off my tongue. I was so used to saying it. But was it still true?

Ja'far's face grew stony. "I should challenge you for the offense you have done me," he said, voice dangerously soft. "I raised both my daughters to be independent, intelligent, and the equal of any man they chose to marry. To perpetually distrust one, like she is naught but a willful child, is inexcusable."

Pain welled up in my chest, matching the rush of tears to my eyes. He was right. Sutaita had respected every request I'd made of her, and I'd repaid that loyalty with lies and dishonesty—the very thing I would have killed her for without a second thought. I was such a hypocrite.

Ja'far saw the regret cross my face and softened his tone. "Shahryar, a man's wife is his partner, his solace in life. Does Sutaita ask you for unreasonable things? Request expensive decorations and clothing? Waste your time and resources with fripperies and silliness?"

Mute, I shook my head.

"Then why would you not want to honor her with your trust? She asks not for your riches, just your regard. Ask any married man, and he will tell you that if all your wife wants is you, then you have a happy marriage indeed."

The self-revulsion consumed me. "Ja'far. I—Allah forgive me, I am not a man, but a villain. I want to stop, I really do, but some days I just—can't."

"Have you talked to Sutaita about this?" He gestured to the parchment. "Explained your past to her?" Ja'far gripped both my shoulders reassuringly.

I shook my head. "No. I—I couldn't. If I tell her this, she may hate me. She may want to leave. She would know too much, be too close." I picked up the letter, hand trembling. "If I tell her, how could she ever trust me? Ever let me touch her?

Ja'far studied me. "You love her."

"Of course I do!" I snapped. "She...she is unlike anyone I have ever known." And now, as the fear of losing her became real, I finally understood how thoroughly she'd stolen my heart.

Nodding, Ja'far paced around me. "Then why have you not reversed your edict?"

Silence sank between us like a stone in water.

"I—I haven't had time." *I was afraid to.*

Ja'far crossed his arms. "You have time now." He started down the hallway.

I hesitated. Once I reversed that, I was stuck, forever. I could not just execute a wife I grew tired of. I would need to make the marriage work. I would have to give up my war on duplicitous women and yield to the incredible and awe-inspiring force that was Scheherazade.

But could I tell her the truth?

Now, as I sat contemplating that threat, I also had the vision of Sutaita kneeling before me, unshed tears pooling in her bistre eyes. It wasn't just Ja'far living in constant fear. Sutaita had given up everything and taken a gamble in hopes of saving her sister.

I had the paperwork drawn up to reverse the edict. Ja'far had dropped it off before departing west to speak with the four upstarts. All I had to do was sign it.

If I signed it, however, I had to tell her the truth. All of it. Even the parts that shamed me most. I played with the pen in my hands, then ruffled other stacks of paper. Anything to put off making this decision.

Because once I told her the truth, she might do the one thing that would ruin me forever. She might leave, and I would be helpless to stop her.

That plain piece of parchment shifted when a breeze blew in from the window. It was as if it struggled to be free and drift away on the wind. That decided me. It was in her name. Freedom—she would give me freedom. I was already learning to let go of my hate. I realized I wasn't losing or surrendering. Instead, I was escaping, fleeing the ghosts and terrors of my past to emerge, healed and new, because of Scherezade.

I didn't even hesitate before signing it and pressing my seal to it. Sutaita had given me herself, and through that gift, given me everything. Now it was my turn to give her life.

One Thousand and One Days

.

Chapter 20
Day 975: Shahryar

Three days ago, I'd celebrated the simple joy of marriage with Sutaita. I'd declared the day a holiday and, instead of holding court, arranged for dancing, poetry, and other entertainment I could share with my wife and her family.

Ja'far had still not returned from the family seat, his base while approaching the four discontented sheikhs. I'd written him after settling the law but told him I didn't want to announce it, not yet, until the threat to my wife was settled.

It also gave me time before I had to tell Sutaita about that and reveal the secret I'd kept to myself for so long.

In the meantime, I'd tried to bridge the gap that had grown between us, but to no avail. Sutaita told her stories dutifully each night, but her heart was no longer in it. Instead of passion, I received a dull recitation. Was it a test? Did she mean to see if I would grow bored and act against her?

I left court a couple hours early. I needed to fix this. I missed her, not just the stories. No one was in my chambers. She must still be studying. I turned around and headed down the hall to her rooms.

She sat in her studying area but at a cushion staring out the window instead of at the table where her books and papers were. There were no tears in her eyes, but the sorrow reflected throughout her countenance weighed heavy on my heart.

Oh, Scheherazade—what have I done to you?

Sutaita had never been effervescent like her sister. Hers was a controlled, calm energy. I adored it. It was soothing, relaxing, to be in her company, and even when her face and eyes came alive in storytelling, she was somehow still approachable.

The person sitting at the window was not the woman I'd grown attached to. This person was someone who had given up. She wasn't holding back each night as a test. She had accepted what was, in her mind, a certain death.

When I realized I had caused her grief, my heart broke.

I could not wait a moment longer.

I cleared my throat. With a start, she looked over and saw me.

"Sutaita, I find myself missing you this day."

A faint blush bloomed in her cheeks.

"Won't you join me in my chambers? I know it's early, but I would like your company."

She collected herself and stood. I offered her my arm to escort her. After a second's hesitation, she took it.

"I never finished telling you about what happened in my first marriage."

If not for the hand on my arm, I would not have felt the merest beat of the pulse on her wrist, the only tell she gave that revealed a reaction to what I'd said. *Please, let it be curiosity and not fear.*

"I wish to set the record straight tonight. I dismissed the servants so we could have privacy. If you need assistance changing later, however—"

"I thank you for your consideration, but I'll be fine." The smile she gave me did not quite reach her eyes.

No trust, not yet. And after what I confided, maybe not ever. *You can still back out of this.* I firmly shoved down that thought. If I dwelt on it, I would lose my nerve from fear of losing my greatest treasure. I'd decided to tell her.

I led her toward the cushions and gestured for her to sit. I joined her, then reached out to trace the side of her face, where the strong cheekbones melded into her thin, ethereal neck. She looked away.

Damn it, Shahryar, what have you done?

It brought the memories of Jathbiyya roaring to the fore of my thoughts. I was failing—failing at loving, driving my wife away. The realization hurt. I had thought myself beyond caring about how any woman thought of me, but then Sutaita happened. I knew then that no matter what, I had to tell her the truth—all of it.

"I had told you that finding my brother's wife in a compromising position reignited the conflict between us. That was a lie. I am sorry for deceiving you, but..." My voice broke. *Please, please, Allah, let her understand.* "What I am about to tell you is something only known to a few other people. Please, do not share it with anyone—not even Dunyazade."

I waited for her to nod before continuing, "After the disastrous confrontation with my brother, I departed the family seat and made for Baghdad. I did have a few other stops to make, so it wasn't as direct a route as I had hoped..."

The return of the sultan to the palace is never a quiet thing. Guards are sent for at the city gates, and they secure a route to the palace, serving as an escort through the city. All of this takes almost an hour, and as the guard is stationed in the palace, all other residents know of the sultan's arrival well before he actually gets there. So no matter what the circumstances may be, my return from an extended journey is never a surprise for anyone.

By the time I actually got into the palace and set foot in my residential wing, I was understandably exhausted. I bypassed my suite for Jathbiyya's. Our fight still bothered me, and I hoped my absence would see me welcomed back with open and forgiving arms.

But her rooms were empty. I looked and called and finally resorted to asking a passing servant if she had seen my wife. The servant looked away quickly before telling me no.

Confused, I headed back toward my rooms. I felt a sense of déjà vu as I approached my bedchamber. Sounds echoed down the hall, noises like those I had heard last at Muhammad's.

I ran down the remainder of the hall and into the room. What I saw horrified me.

My brother was on top of my wife, without a stitch of clothing on, thrusting into her. Her eyes were shut, and her arms gripped him tightly, urging him on. Muhammad heard me come in, looked at me, and smiled, his eyes gleaming with a cruel glint.

Bile rose in my throat. I tried to speak, to say something to stop the horrible image in front of me, but could not make my voice work. As I struggled, I also realized that four other men stood in the room watching. Four witnesses. My wife would be tried and found guilty of adultery, no matter how I felt.

Feeling sick, I rushed out of the room. I barely made it to a nearby window before emptying the contents of my stomach. It didn't matter, because I still felt nauseated as I collapsed down. Tears sprang to my eyes. Why? How could he do this to me?

It was at that moment that I remembered the last encounter with Muhammad in his garden. *I want you to suffer as I have.* And, apparently, he had wasted no time ensuring that I would suffer.

Sorrow threatened to overcome me as I considered Jathbiyya. Not only was she unfaithful, but it had seemed as though she was willing, eager to betray me. I knew things between us were bad, but this? What had I ever done to deserve such betrayal from her?

You put the kingdom first, a little voice in the back of my head told me. *Women always want to be first, always want to be the most. You insulted her in the worst way possible.* But I had promised her love—eternal, lasting love. If she returned that love in any way, she would not have been able to do this to me.

I resolved to discover the truth. I squared my shoulders, pushed myself up, and marched to the guard station.

The lieutenant on duty saw me approach and came to attention.

"Lieutenant, I need to know when Muhammad arrived in Baghdad and at the palace."

"Of course, Your Majesty." He consulted a scroll, then discarded it for another. He then announced, "Prince Muhammad arrived yesterday in the early morning. The guard on duty noted that he seemed tired and dusty from travel, concluding that he had ridden through the night in order to arrive by that time. When queried about his business, he told the guard that he was a prince and could come and go as he pleased. The guard decided to admit him." The lieutenant rerolled the scroll, returning it to the shelf. "Is there anything else I can do, Majesty?"

Jathbiyya had told me to be less honest, that I needed to anticipate the deceit of others.

I met the guard's gaze coldly. "My brother and my wife are in my chamber. They are to be arrested immediately—for adultery."

The lieutenant saluted again, face impassive, then gestured to a nearby detachment of guards and motioned for them to follow him. I considered following as well, but decided instead to go to the throne room. Their arrest would be as good a reason as any to hold court immediately.

I had barely settled in my seat when four guardsmen entered with Jathbiyya. The witnesses and my brother were nowhere to be seen.

I stood. "Where is Muhammad?"

One guard saluted. "He was not there, Majesty. Only the sultana was there, and she refused to come willingly."

My mind raced. What about those witnesses? Once I saw how many there were, it made perfect sense. According to the Qur'an, four witnesses needed to testify to prove adultery. In the absence of Muhammad and the others, there was no case against Jathbiyya—save what I chose to enact as the sultan. And now the witnesses—and Muhammad—were gone.

I struggled to consider the potential deceit. If I ever learned anything from Jathbiyya, it would be this—to start considering the possible deception of others. Four witnesses...and four directions. Muhammad had probably already dispatched them to spread the news of the adultery of the sultana. His name would not be mentioned, of course. Utter fury overtook me.

"Lock her in a cell for questioning." I stood and strode out of the throne room. Seething, I returned to my chamber and slammed the door shut. The maids had been fast at work—the bed had already been stripped and remade, leaving no trace of the illicit activity. I screamed and punched the wall.

Everything was falling apart. My wife, whom I had loved with everything in me, had completely and utterly betrayed me for my brother—the brother who also turned on me, his family, the moment I came between him and the power he craved. I had hoped to salvage that relationship and become a family again. Instead, I was awarded pain and suffering. With Jathbiyya, I only sought to balance my duty and responsibility to my empire with those of being a husband. Instead of returning the loving support I gave her, she betrayed me as well.

In fact, everyone in my life who was close to me had tricked me with lies in one way or another. Even my father, waiting until the last possible moment to name me heir, cheated me out of the education and experience I needed to be the best ruler I could be. Jathbiyya had been absolutely right about one thing: the only way to get ahead, the only way to ensure that I was never fooled and hurt again, was to plan on the manipulative behavior of others and take no qualms with lying myself to get what I wanted.

I took several long moments to just breathe. My rage cooled, but the hatred inside me solidified like ice.

I left Jathbiyya in that dungeon for a week. During that time, messengers were dispatched, the army recalled, and scouts and recruiters sent into Muhammad's territory to learn what they could while draining his province of able-bodied men.

Every time I began to regret my actions, wonder if I was being too hasty, if I should forgive, I thought of Jathbiyya in that dungeon. All my worries would harden into a well-stoked fury instead.

When I finally descended to see her, Jathbiyya was completely changed from the woman I knew. Her magical smile was gone, replaced by thin lips and pale countenance. She had lost weight, and the prison guard informed me that she had been refusing to eat. I wasn't sure what was waiting for me. Would she beg forgiveness? Dangle her infidelity in front of me and laugh? When she noticed me, she looked away, anger flashing in her eyes.

"Jathbiyya, I am here to find answers to questions. If you agree to be honest, it will be easier for you."

She snorted. "I will still die. How could you make that easier?"

I took a deep breath. I would not let her succeed, I would keep my calm. "According to the law, I can have you stoned. If you cooperate, I can make your death faster and relatively painless."

She rolled away from me to lie on her side, facing the wall. "Why bother? You have made up your mind. Nothing I say will change it."

That feeling arose in me again. Despite her decrepit appearance, despite her betrayal, Allah help me, I still loved her. I felt the pressure of my decision come to bear. This was the moment: would I acquiesce and forgive, or take the lesson and punish her?

The vision of her with my brother returned to my head. No, this I could never forgive. I would see her dead, feeling physically the pain she inflicted emotionally on me. But I could not let her know it. I needed to know why so I could have that closure and move on with my life.

I would need to lie.

Thankfully, she had taught me how.

"Jathbiyya, I swore to love you—unconditionally. If I could spare you this, I would."

She rolled back over, her eyes boring into mine. "You would free me? And forgive me?"

I nodded.

She rolled back toward the wall. "I don't believe you."

Time to show her that I had learned how to deceive. "I am not the one who has lied here. In fact, my desire to be honest has led me to be the injured party here." The volume of my voice rose. "You have been provided food, water, everything you need, yet you refuse to partake. You are punishing yourself. Do not try to frame me in your connivance!"

During my speech, she had hugged her knees, rolling into a little ball. When I finished, she gradually unfolded and sat up, facing me. Her head hung down, and crystalline drops fell from her eyes to wet the floor. "Do you love me? Like you said? No matter what?"

The pleading tone of her voice pierced my heart. I wanted to say yes and mean it. I wanted to forgive and forget. *Remember: she taught you about lying. She will always lie. Even this, these tears, are lies.*

So I lied right back. "Of course I do, sweet. But I can't just let this go. There were witnesses. If I can't find them, the scandal threatens the country and threatens you. If I were to lose you—I can't even imagine."

She wiped the tears from her face. "Oh, Shahryar—I did it for you—for us."

I was too new to intrigue for this. I know my eyes narrowed in confusion. "How did you think that adultery, a grave sin, would be good for us?"

"I—I knew we needed a child. An heir. When Muhammad approached me, I thought it would s-s-solve our p-p-p-problems." The tears returned full stream.

She must be lying. She had to be. What woman, what Muslim, would even consider adultery? It was a crime punishable by death. And to interfere with inheritance, purposefully seek to carry another man's child...I could not even fathom her reasoning.

"Just to make sure I understand, sweet—you were trying to fix our conception problems?"

She nodded.

"What if the problem is that you are barren—what then? Would you have cuckolded me for a year? Two? How long?" My anger rose

Her face drained of color.

"How long?" I thundered.

"I— I— I d-d-don't know." She threw herself from the bench and collapsed on the floor. "Shahryar, believe me, forgive me, I didn't think, I just felt so hurt that you cared more about the empire than me. You would have it spread about that we were b-b-b-barren!" She clutched at the bars separating us. "You have to believe me! I never wanted to hurt you. I wanted to make you happy, I w-w-wanted a family with you."

Emotions raced around my head, around my heart. I understood too well doing the wrong thing for the right reason—such decisions had comprised the majority of dealings with my brother. Her anguish beat at my defenses. I would give anything to make this better—because I had told her truly: I would never stop loving her.

She was right that I loved the empire and its people more, that I loved my title, my position, and the responsibility it entailed more. Maybe I always had, which was why I could understand and justify Muhammad's anger at me supplanting him.

"Sweet, I want to forgive and forget. But I need to know what Muhammad's plan is. I need to know where those witnesses are. Because as the sultan, I cannot ignore the law. You know this."

She nodded.

"Where are they? Help me to help you."

She breathed in a shuddering breath. "He told me that they were for my protection, in case you grew angry. I knew he was lying, but I thought that if it got out, you would step down, cede the empire to him, so we could be together, just us." She looked right at me, and by the clarity in her eyes I knew, for the first time in our acquaintance, that she was being honest with me. "They are riding in each direction. In a month's time, once Muhammad has gathered an army, they will announce what they witnessed." She looked away. "You returned too soon. Too soon, and now everything is ruined."

I had my information. Now it was time to drop the ax on her. "Thank you, Jathbiyya. I must correct you, however, sweet."

She looked up at the dripping sarcasm of the last word, startled.

"You ruined everything when you were selfish and chose yourself before me. I made you sultana so you could choose this Empire first. I treated you with ultimate love and kindness, and you threw it away to serve your own ambitions."

I returned to the stair door and rapped three times. A magistrate and two guards appeared. "As sultan, I sentence her to death immediately. She is a liar and an adulteress. For her service," I said insinuatingly, "she is granted a quick death: beheading."

Jathbiyya sat there in shock, speechless. When I finished my proclamation, she screamed one single word: "*No!*"

Sutaita sat as still as if she'd been frozen. Her amber skin was ashen.

"I didn't want to tell you because I was ashamed. Ashamed that she lowered me so." I reached out a hand. *Please, let her understand. I need her to understand.*

Sutaita took it. "I know you said in the past you don't want sympathy or pity. But by Allah! How horrible!" She shook her head. "I cannot believe one partner would do that to the other."

I waited a minute, letting her process my story. The sorrow and understanding on her face were honest, earnest. In comforting me, she let slip the mask of coolness she wore so often. It was the same as when she told her stories, when she let her guard down. I remembered the honesty I'd treasured before. Could it be that she felt the same? That open, genuine communication allowed us to connect, to understand each other, to love each other?

I spoke again, "There is more, but if you are willing, I would tell you at another time."

She nodded. "May I...may I hug you?"

Relief broke over me like a splash of cold water. "Yes. I would like that."

One Thousand and One Days

Chapter 21
Day 996: Sulaila

I reeled after Shahryar's revelation. He had done what he needed to, both as a husband and a ruler. But something still bothered me. Those four witnesses and his brother. Clearly, Shahryar had stopped the news somehow, else the general population would have known of the scandal.

I wanted to ask my father about it, for surely, he knew the details, but he was still away on some sort of trip for Shahryar. Father had been short on details when he left, and Shahryar had dodged my questions when I asked. Despite how far we'd come, his lack of trust still irked me.

I paced in my room, thinking on the problem. For all the progress I'd made on solving the puzzle that was Shahryar, I still didn't know the final piece: why he'd turned around and vowed to slaughter each new wife.

Armed with new information, I wanted to re-read the history of the Byzantine war. But Shahryar had become extremely strict with any sort of excursion around the same time my father left, making getting any new materials difficult. Dunyazade had been staying in the palace, rather than alone at Father's house, and she was not exempt from Shahryar's outside travel ban.

I paused, finger tapping my chin as I thought. Were the two related? I dismissed that thought. Shahryar had always been overprotective, and with my father gone, he apparently took protecting Dunyazade seriously.

I couldn't do research, and I couldn't talk to Dunyazade about it because I was sworn to secrecy. I couldn't ask Father about it, for he was away. And Shahryar refused to speak of it at all. My fists clenched in frustration.

I considered visiting Khaizuran, but as I had just gone yesterday, that was not an option. I asked after Dunyazade, but she'd been feeling poorly yesterday, and the maid told me that she was abed, resting.

After pacing my room for an hour in boredom, I decided I had had enough of this captivity. I was a sultana, or so everyone told me. Shouldn't I have the freedom to leave if I wished? Part of me dreaded risking Shahryar's wrath, but my restlessness quickly silenced it.

Mirko and Rumi were nowhere to be seen. That was odd. The pair usually stood outside my door at all times, trading off guard duty for breaks as needed. I took it as an omen. I should leave this prison.

As I wandered the corridors, I considered visiting the archives. I could double-check the names of those guards, maybe solve that one part of the puzzle. I felt certain that they were the witnesses and that their ascendancy to the nobility was the price of their silence. I started down to the gallery, intent on my plan.

In the hall, studying the painting of Shahryar, a strange sheikh stood. I didn't think much of it—sheikhs regularly came to visit Shahryar in the palace, and although I had never seen one in this wing, surely, he would not be here if it were not allowed.

The man turned as I drew near. He smiled. The light line of a scar scored one cheek, a glint of something indeterminate shining in his eyes. "Sultana. What a pleasure to see you here...alone."

I swallowed, trying to ease the lump of nervousness growing in my throat. The scar helped me recognize the man. He was one of the four. I usually marveled at how our brains worked, remembering information when presented with a cue. This was not one of those times. "Sheikh Bijan. I did not know you were in Baghdad."

His hand snaked out and grabbed my wrist.

I jerked my arm back. No success. "Unhand me."

His smile iced over. "No, Sutaita, I don't think I will." He strode down the hall, dragging me behind him.

My heart turned into a lump of icy fear.

"Parham and Shadan have seen to your guards, and Jahan was waiting near the seraglio. Lucky me, you felt like reading today."

I felt as though a large rock had appeared in my stomach. The voices of the concubines echoed in my ears. *Remember, the sheikhs Jahan, Parham, Shadan, and Bijan are visiting. The guards are always lax when they're in town.*

"You made certain Mirko and Rumi were gone."

Bijan laughed. "It was too easy. Once a soldier, always a soldier." He glanced over a well-muscled shoulder. "But you wouldn't know anything about that, would you, Sutaita?"

This conversation was getting me nowhere. "Where are you taking me?"

We paused at the end of the corridor. Bijan's eyes flicked over me, considering. "Away. Shahryar would do anything to get you back. So away, until we have what we want."

I pulled against his grip, to no avail. My mind raced. They had taken part in a plot against the sultan. Instead of execution, he'd granted them land and titles. "What more could you possibly want? You've been elevated from a common soldier to a sheikh." Besides, this man couldn't possibly know that Shahryar would easily forget about me. And if he learned...my heart froze in horror.

Ignoring my struggles, Bijan studied the stone wall in front of us, then moved aside a tapestry and pressed a button. The wall swung out, revealing a simple corridor. The servant's paths.

Bijan sneered as he hustled me into the hidden passage. "What else? More land, more power. Besides, Shahryar has had this coming for a long time."

I renewed my struggles, hoping to slow him down. "How could the sultan have had this coming? What did he ever do to you, besides raise your fortunes?" I had to distract him, slow him down.

Hand tightening on my arm, Bijan pulled me close until our noses nearly touched. His dark brown eyes glittered malevolently. "I lost family—brothers-at-arms—in all the wars the stupid sultan caused. He could have stepped aside and let Muhammad rule. Instead, Shahryar fought him twice, and Byzantium as well. Gold, silks, perfumes, land—none of that could ever repay the blood debt on the sultan's head.

"Besides, Shahryar knows we're coming for you. We sent him a letter more than a month ago. Instead of paying, he sent that snake, Ja'far, to try to appease us." Bijan snorted. "As if we could trust anything that came out of that man's mouth."

I bristled. "That man is my father!"

Bijan threw his head back and laughed out loud at this. "That makes this too perfect! Ja'far won't advise Shahryar to ignore threats and ransom—not when the vizier wants his daughter back."

I ignored anything else Bijan said. I had to find a way out of this. I could tell that he was leading me toward the edge of the palace. They probably meant to whisk me right out from under Shahryar's nose. So I needed to escape before we left the grounds. Looking about, the passage was astonishingly empty. I had hoped to find tools or anything that might have been handy to grab as a weapon. Alas, luck was not with me in that area.

That left only my hijab. Tears sprang to my eyes. The best way to save my life would be to reveal my hair and neck to this...this monster.

No. This I could not do. There had to be another way.

Time. That's what I needed. Time for Shahryar to notice me missing, time for Mirko and Rumi to return to their post. And now, after nearly two and a half years, I was an expert at stalling for time. "What makes you think the sultan cares for me?"

"You're alive, aren't you?" Bijan stopped short, eyeing me with suspicion. "Not one maid survived until you." His hand still clenched my wrist too tight.

I winced.

"How did you change him?" Bijan asked. "It's the one thing I never understood. You're not much to look at, and Ja'far would not allow any...ill-repute...to come to his daughter."

I swallowed my indignation at the veiled insult. He clearly meant to bait me, just as Shahryar had for most of the first year of our marriage.

"You really want to know?" I asked softly, hoping he'd think me cowed.

A sly smile snaked across his face. "Yes. Tell me. Better yet, show me, Sultana."

I swallowed down the nausea his lust-filled eyes awoke in me and launched into the story of me and Shahryar, hoping against hope it would distract and slow Bijan. I told him of my decision to sacrifice myself to save my sister. His grip softened at that. He hadn't been lying about taking this action for revenge. Sensing his interest, I explained about Dunyazade and how we'd both grown up without a mother. Mayhap if I could win over his sympathies, he'd drop the plan.

When I mentioned Shahryar and his cold, unfettered rage, Bijan threw his head back and laughed. "And how long, little Sultana, did it take for you to realize he'd fallen in love with you?"

I prayed that months of practice in cool, collected countenance would pay off now. The sheikh was wrong. Shahryar didn't love me. We'd grown closer, but not as a husband and wife. For all I knew, Bijan and his cronies were merely saving Shahryar the trouble of explaining the resumption of spousal executions.

Bijan's eyes narrowed at my silence.

I had to tell the story. "My lord, he does not love me. You are mistaken. We may care for a beloved object, but we cannot love it, not as we would a person."

He laughed at this, the sound echoing down the corridor. "You truly don't know, do you? If I had a conscience, I'd feel simply awful now." He laughed again, but I heard another sound underneath the resonating guffaw.

Mirko, Rumi, and a contingent of other guards came charging down the servant's paths, tackling Bijan. His fall wrenched my arm, and I cried out in pain—the former soldier hadn't released me before tumbling down.

"My lady, come quickly." Mirko escorted me away. "The sultan is beside himself with worry."

I stumbled alongside, feeling numb. I'd done it. For whatever reason, I felt stuck, as though part of me wished Mirko had been a few minutes later, as though his arrival kept some secret truth from me. I blinked my eyes against the bright light of the main palace hall as we exited the tunnels.

Shahryar paced the hallway, face pale. When he saw me, he rushed over. "Sutaita!" He grabbed my chin and studied my face with one hand, the other stroking down my head to my shoulders. Seeing no marks or bruises, he squeezed me to his chest in a tight hug. "Praise Allah! I thought I'd lost you."

I felt the rapid beat of his heart on my chest. He'd actually been worried about me.

Shahryar pulled away. "Mirko. Rumi. Escort Sutaita back to her rooms."

I could tell from the thunderous expression on the Shah's face that all three of us were in trouble. Instead of arguing, I followed the two guards back to the family suite. None of us spoke a word.

"We'll be standing right outside, my lady." Rumi gave me a polite bow before darting out the door.

I sank down into a nearby cushion with a sigh.

It didn't take long for Shahryar to walk calmly into my room. He stood in the entryway, staring me down.

After several long minutes, he burst out, "You should not have gone alone. Why do you defy me?"

I took a deep breath. I could not answer his anger with anger. "My lord, you never said..."

"You should have known!" He stalked past me, fists clenched.

I tried again, fighting to keep temper out of my voice. "You never informed me..."

"You should know!" He whirled about to face me. His face was purple with anger.

"How?" I finally shouted back, rising to my feet. "How should I know when you won't tell me anything?"

He strode up to me, stopping only once we were standing toe to toe. His volume dropped to a dangerous low. "I tell you all that you need to know!"

"Then when did you ever tell me that I could not leave my rooms alone?"

He seemed about to retort but stopped. This happened two more times before he threw his hands in the air. "You stupid woman."

I raised my chin. "My lord, I am not stupid. You cannot blame me for the actions of another, whether it be a derelict member of your court or any of the dozens of wives you have had."

Something entered his eyes. It almost looked like...fear. He gripped the table, his hands shaking. He stared me down, fury still etched on his face. "You deliberately put yourself in danger."

"What do you care? The only reason you keep me alive is to hear the end of a story."

That time, I recognized what flashed through his eyes. Hurt. He raised a hand, and I braced myself for a blow, shutting my eyes tight and wincing. After a moment, when nothing happened, I squinted. He had left.

I was stupid. To ruin everything over the need to be right...I should have just apologized and kept quiet. Why hadn't I? Why did I forget myself and become emotional?

I thought about the past months—we had grown closer. He had gentled somewhat. Maybe I forgot...but did I love him? Could he ever love me? I closed my eyes. It seemed impossible. *Of course it's impossible when you use your gift of words to wound him so.* I should never have spoken that aloud. I had surely decimated any straggling seedling of love that could exist between us.

I resigned myself to the consequences of losing my temper. I knew I needed to remain detached, remain dispassionate. I had failed.

That evening, even though I was not summoned to his chamber, I went anyway. He was standing by the window, staring out over the city.

"I'm sorry." I could not even find a way to say it eloquently.

"I know." He sighed and looked toward me. "I was too hard on you. I have been too hard on you, keeping you here like this. But when I heard..."

I peered in his eyes. I did not know the ghosts that haunted him. "Maybe I should go."

"No." He shuddered as if feeling a draft of cold air. "No, please stay and tell some more about Ma'aruf the Cobbler and his wife."

"Are you certain?"

"I know my anger frightens you. But spending time with you, like this, it helps. It helps me so much." He turned, and his eyes pleaded with mine. "Please, Scherezade."

One Thousand and One Days

Chapter 22
Day 999: Shahryar

It took me over two days before I could talk to Sutaita again.

I still listened to her stories each night, still said all the prayers with her, still ate breakfast with her after morning prayers.

I just didn't say a word to her.

I couldn't believe how naive she'd been. Sutaita was a smart woman. She knew the risk inherent with my rank and her position. She knew I wanted to protect her.

Or did she?

I racked my brains, trying to remember what I'd done after receiving the ransom notice from those four ungrateful wretches. I'd sent Ja'far away, notified Sutaita's guard, curtailed our excursions...

But I never told Sutaita. It was as though I'd been punched in the stomach. Sutaita was smart but not omnipotent. All she saw was her father leaving and a change in me. How scared she must have been. And how easily the entire fiasco could have been avoided. Had I trusted Sutaita, confided in her about the letter, worked with her, she would have known the risk, recognized the danger when her guards weren't there.

My blood boiled remembering that. Shadan and Parham used their former relationships with the guard to distract Mirko and Rumi. They'd been planning this for a while, it seemed. Sutaita had begged for me to forgive the two deserters, but they were still imprisoned. They had known there was a risk, just not the source.

With a sigh, I sank into the hard wooden chair behind my desk. I probably should have been more forthright with them as well. It was strange how the very thing that I thought would make me safe—keeping secrets—nearly cost me everything. I picked up the small note sitting on the corner of my desk. It was from Sutaita, sent over a year ago on an especially beautiful day, asking me to go into Baghdad with her and visit the House of Wisdom. I'd kept it there ever since. Re-reading it, I smiled. Compared to Jathbiyya, Sutaita didn't ask much. All she ever seemed to want were small moments with me, time to learn and grow together, to share in the everyday pleasures of life, and the chance to continue being herself.

I carefully set the note down. I knew what I had to do. I couldn't risk keeping any secret from Sutaita any longer. This last one...when I thought about what could have happened, my heart froze in horror. I could have lost her forever.

That decided me. I had to tell her the whole truth. If she hated me for it, so be it. But I could not continue loving her and lying to her. I could not take the chance that my secrets could cost her her life.

I found her bent over a book in her room. Other than slightly raised eyebrows, she evinced no sign of surprise at my presence. I couldn't keep from smiling. Even after everything, she still kept herself cool, collected, and in control. How had I ever seen that as icy? It wasn't a cold rejection, but a passion of logic, of removing emotional expressions from conversations. Someone I could trust with anything, because she would not be coerced into betraying me by anything.

"You asked about my brother, how he died."

Sutaita nodded.

"Please, sit. I will tell you everything. The wars I sought to avoid lasted almost two years. Muhammad sold and bartered away every shred of honor he had left. Every time I thought he could sink no lower, he did." And I relived the worst memory of my life.

It had been early morning. I had already breakfasted and was in council with the general and some other military attendants. Ja'far would often handle administrative work for me, so when he burst into the council room, I was surprised.

"Your Majesty." He bowed. "I must discuss something with you and your councilors immediately."

I gestured to a seat. "Of course. Please."

Ja'far walked to the chair but did not sit. He hesitated. "Your Majesty, I was approached regarding my eldest daughter. I was offered a marriage agreement with the sultan—in exchange for spying on you for Muhammad."

The sweet, icy-cold anger spread from my heart and filled my veins. "You are certain?"

"Yes. But before I refuse, I have an idea."

Even the soldiers looked interested now.

"I accept his offer but insist that the wedding take place before I agree to anything. He will accept because physically having my daughter would make me more agreeable to his—" Ja'far's mouth wrinkled in disgust "—requests."

I nodded slowly, understanding the scheme.

"Instead of actually sending my daughter, we send a trained assassin. We kill your brother, and with him, this rebellion, in one easy stroke."

The soldiers clapped at this. After almost a year of fighting, they wanted peace restored. We also had a war declaration from Byzantium to deal with.

"Do as you see fit, Ja'far. You have my permission and my trust. But one thing—bring him to me alive."

Ja'far bowed and left the room.

It took over two months for Ja'far's trap to spring its jaws shut. I was awakened late at night with news that a prisoner had arrived, and my attendance was urgently needed. As I dressed, Ja'far himself arrived and confirmed my suspicions.

"We have him, Your Majesty. He is in the dungeon under heavy guard."

I nodded as I finished straightening my clothes. I wanted to be dressed as a king. I wanted my brother's last image to be me, triumphing over him. Then, maybe, I could trust again. Maybe I could return to being Shahryar and stop having to choose between being the ruthless sultan and a caring family member.

From the depths of his cell, Muhammad sneered at me. "Look at my wonderful big brother—descended from on high to mingle with humanity. How goes the empire, Brother?"

I would not let him bait me. I had won. He was the last traitor, and with his death, I could be free. Free of worry, free of the bonds that tore at my allegiances.

"Let's not waste time. Muhammad al-Amin, you are accused of several grave crimes. First, you are a traitor to the empire and a false pretender to the throne—"

Muhammad sputtered. "Pretender? I am—"

"According to the last wishes of the previous ruler, Shahryar al'Ma-mun, or myself, was named total heir of the Abbasid Empire. In defiance of that edict, you have committed several treasonous acts, including the imprisonment of the rightful sultan—"

"Just a—"

"Conspiracy to violate a peace treaty with Byzantium,"

"Wait, that's not—"

"Adultery and grave sexual crimes against the wife of the sultan—"

"*No!*"

"And rebellion against the appointed ruler." I took a deep breath. "How do you plead?"

"Not guilty!" he snarled. "You have no witnesses for any of this! You can't prove anything!"

I nodded. "Guard, please bring the witnesses."

One of the guards bowed and left. Silence stretched over the room.

"You don't have any witnesses, Shahryar. Face it. You lost. You will never find the information you need to execute me." Arrogance marred his face. "You should let me go and abdicate. You were never meant for the throne—you are too soft, too trusting."

I chuckled under my breath. "Let's wait and see what the witnesses say."

Concern flitted across his face. His features rearranged themselves into condescending contempt. "We both know you have no witnesses. Stop this charade, Brother."

"Out of the two of us claiming to have won this contest, I am not the one locked in a cell."

His eyes flashed with anger at that. He opened his mouth to speak, but the creaking door and entrance of the guard with four men stopped him. The look on my brother's face as he recognized Jahan, Parham, Shadan, and Bijan was priceless.

"These men, Brother, are the witnesses I procured." I turned to face the witnesses. "Please give your testimony."

Jahan stepped forward. "Your Majesty, I did witness this man in the cell commit a sexual crime with the late sultana."

Parham stepped forward. "As did I."

"And I," from Shadan.

"And I." The testimony of Bijan sealed Muhammad's fate.

"No! *No!* These are lies! They give false testimony! Shahryar, please!" Muhammad fell on his knees, begging. "Shahryar, my brother, you—you can't do this! You never lie! Please! Shahryar, please—no!"

"Muhammad al-Amin, you are convicted of the accused crimes. The sentencing for these crimes, on all accounts, is death. I will consider the method and return to see justice done." I breathed out. It was done. "Any last words before I make my deliberations?"

"I-I...she lied, Shahryar. She lied to both of us. It was her idea all along; she wanted the power. And I—I couldn't stop once I started! She was certain you wouldn't kill her, said you loved her."

I stood as still as a statue as he rained poison down on my ears.

"It was never supposed to come to this. You were supposed to abdicate. You swore you loved her. And she was going to kill you and take care of it all." He looked right into my eyes, beseechingly. "Please, you have to believe me."

"My deliberations are complete. Behead him. Immediately."

The guards opened the cell door and swarmed Muhammad, holding him down. One guard left and returned with a specially sharpened ax. The ax whistled through the air before thudding into the floor, severing my brother's head from his body.

I turned and left while my brother's lifeblood streamed out of his twitching body.

Now Sutaita knew the truth. Indeed, she was already gathering herself, adjusting her understanding of me to accommodate the information I shared. It was as if everything was a puzzle to her. I wondered if she would ever see me as a person, as flesh and blood, with emotions, fears, desires, ambitions—and if she would ever drop that wall and let me see her that way as well.

For myself, I felt an enormous sense of relief. Keeping this from everyone had taken such a toll on me. Since I had interrogated Jathbiyya in private, no one knew about the most private matters. Now the woman I cared about knew. No matter what happened, I had come home. I had found the honesty I abandoned. And I wanted, more than anything, to be able to share the trust with Sutaita that Jathbiyya had spurned.

Sutaita was not yet satisfied. I could tell by the way she held herself, in perfect control, despite appearing relaxed. "My heart grieves for you, my lord. I understand now why my independence tested your limits. But I don't understand—why all other women?"

"Looking back, it seems so foolish, so wasteful," I admitted. I wished I'd had a better response. I should have prepared myself for that question.

A spark of fire flashed in her eyes. "Wasteful?" Her lips thinned, and she seemed about to speak, then thought the better of it and turned away.

"There is more," I began.

She shook her head. "I want to be alone."

My heart felt as though it might break. I had hoped she would understand, that the past would help her understand. Had I erred?

"As you wish, my wife." I fought the urge to run to her, to hold her, assure her that I was changed, was different because of her. That I loved her in a way that made what I'd felt for Jathbiyya seem false and hollow. Instead, I left.

Chapter 23
Day 1000: Shahryar

Sutaita's reserve hurt more than I thought possible. Even after witnessing the ultimate betrayal of my first wife, something about Sutaita's quiet censure ripped me apart.

I had disappointed her. I had given in to base emotions, something she never did. She would never respect me, not after that. Love was clearly out of the question.

Although I knew in my heart I should not expect love to be part of a royal marriage, the slow bloom of feelings between us made me hope that this time, it would be different.

Feeling lost and unsure of what to do, I sought out my mother.

I approached the eunuch standing guard at the seraglio. "I'm here to see my mother. Please clear the room. I don't want any, um, distractions."

The eunuch nodded and bowed low before entering the seraglio. He returned a few moments later. "The girls have all taken to their private rooms and will stay there until I bid them, or else suffer the pain of death."

I pursed my lips rather than answer and entered the room. Was I truly that horrible that everyone threatened death on my behalf?

The incense braziers were open, and the sweet and heady scent of vanilla, sandalwood, and cloves permeated the air. The girls had left rapidly, leaving behind wraps and other objects scattered about the cushions on the floor. My mother stood at the doorway to her suite of rooms, leaning against the frame, holding a teacup. She was dressed modestly but left her hair unveiled.

She took a sip from the cup. Lowering it, she murmured my name. "Shahryar, so good to see you."

"And for me to see you." I followed her back to her rooms. There were tea and snacks laid out, but clearly for an earlier visitor. Eyeing the spread, I asked her, "Sutaita?"

"Who else?" She gracefully knelt, then arranged her limbs on the cushions. Patting one next to her, she invited me to join her.

There was nothing I could do but slump down on the cushion and grudgingly accept the offered cup of tea. My mother had always insisted I learn manners, and expected to be treated like a sultana, no matter what her actual status was.

She also knew how to dangle me like a cat does a mouse. "You haven't told Sutaita that you rescinded that edict."

Having no good answer, I sipped my tea and held my tongue.

"Do you remember our conversation after you signed that disgusting law?"

I pressed my lips together. "Yes, Mother. I remember. But why bring that up now?"

"Because you needed to be reminded."

I frowned. "I have repented of my actions. I am trying—failing sometimes, but genuinely trying—to be different. Why do you feel you must remind me?"

"Because you are ruining your chance at true happiness. Sutaita knows you haven't been honest with her. And if you do not confide in her, and soon, you may lose any chance of redemption in her eyes."

"Mother, she already hates me. I told her about Jathbiyya and Muhammed. She's drawn away from me. It's like she's there but only partway. Part of her is somewhere else, somewhere I can never reach."

My mother, damn her soul, laughed. "You really are besotted with her, aren't you?"

I could feel heat creeping over my neck and face. "No more than is reasonable."

"Oh, my son." She moved next to me and pulled me into a hug. "Love is not reasonable. However, it does require honesty. Your father was always perfectly honest about what he could offer me. It freed me to love him because I knew I could trust him. It freed me to choose him because I knew what I was choosing. And it freed him to return my affections because he knew he could bestow them without worry about what I might do."

I began to wonder if maybe I had been right all along, before Jathbiyya and my brother had destroyed me. If maybe, just maybe, honesty could be valued.

Sutaita was honest with me. She was a little headstrong and too independent by far. For her, however, it worked. She didn't need to lie, because she chased after what she wanted. Or she had, until me. For a girl with the nickname freedom, she had endured more imprisonment than anyone I knew.

As I thought, I realized what I needed to do, why I had to relive this horror and tell her. She had to know. I was healing more and more every day, thanks to her. I would also always have those doubts—some of them would never go away.

I would repay her integrity with my own. I would tell her the entire truth, even the moments that I was not proud of.

I just hoped, at the end of it, she would love me as I had grown to love her.

"Thank you, Mother. You always know what to say."

"Of course. I am always here for you." She hesitated a moment. "There is something else you should know. Sutaita's stories—"

My throat constricted. "What about them?" I forced out.

"When she learned that it was either her or Dunyazade who must marry you, she decided to try to prolong her life, that she might discover how to save her sister, if not herself. She did plot with Dunyazade, but only to get you to start listening to the stories, that you would stay the execution."

I fought the anger rising inside me. "I suspected as much. It's one of the things that held me back, kept me from being open with her. It made her seem just like Jathbiyya."

My mother sipped some tea before answering. "Does that make you question your trust in her?"

I stood and began pacing. I had too much energy to sit still. "You just went on about trust and honesty. She's hidden this from me since our marriage began. How does that beget an honest and loving relationship?"

My mother shook her head. "Do you really think that finding a way to stay alive is lying? Tell me, has Sutaita ever used her relationship with you to get something? Political advantage, for example?"

I halted and thought. She had used the family name to access the archives. But she'd done that to try to figure me out, puzzle out my edict, and... "No. The only thing she's ever used her connection with me for was to research and learn a way to save her own life. I—I don't think I can fault her for that." As I said it, I knew it to be true. And I knew in that moment, in my heart, that had I trusted her from the beginning, Sutaita would have immediately returned that trust. After nearly three years with her, I could feel certain about that.

I had grown in these past years to love her. I loved her not with the passionate fire I experienced with Jathbiyya, but with something deeper, like the still water of the deepest lake. How could I tell her? How could I possibly explain everything?

She just wanted to survive. It was harmless. All she had done was preserve her life—how was that at all unexpected?

"Please excuse me, Mother."

"Of course, my son. I expect you will find your wife in the gardens."

With a murmured thanks, I departed.

I found Sutaita in the gardens, as my mother had said. She sat staring blankly at a water fountain. Without her usual mask on, I grimaced inwardly at the pain and hurt written clearly across her features. I didn't deserve her. How many times had I professed that I would tell the truth, the whole of it, and still held something back to ease my own conscience? How could I ever hope to win her trust?

I approached her. "Sutaita, I—that is, I—what I have to tell you now is not easy." I took a deep breath and blew it out. "You deserve to know this. So I will tell you. Just as I promised—that you might know what I really am, and what this marriage really means."

She nodded. Her lips were parted slightly, trembling. I could pull her to me and kiss her senseless. I could demand that she yield, force from her the love I knew was there. Yet even as I thought these things, I knew that it would never be enough. I never wanted to be that person again, the person who took instead of giving, demanded instead of asking.

"As you know, my brother claimed that Jathbiyaa had been behind the entire plot. Her idea was to guilt me into abdicating the throne and then convince me to either fake my own death or kill me herself. She was already dead, and once my brother's sentence was carried out, there was no way to learn the absolute truth." One last time, I allowed my memories to direct me to my dark past.

For three days after Muhammad's execution, I fasted, wept, and prayed. I was all alone. I had no family left. Ja'far tried to remind me of my mother, but I couldn't bear to go and see her. What would she think of me, of the blood on my hands, all because I had been too stupid, too naively trusting, to realize that I had nursed a brood of vipers to my bosom?

On the dawn of the fourth day, I gave in to my aching stomach and broke my fast. Ja'far was in constant attendance, checking on me. He had basically run the kingdom while I grieved. When I showed signs of recovery, he directed me toward simple tasks, as though I were a child. Bathing and dressing, eating and walking, reading a book—that was the sum of my existence for another week.

By then, I was no longer grieving. I was angry. And this anger consumed me like nothing I had ever experienced before. Everything in my life began to pale next to imagining how to exact revenge on two dead people. And as time passed, my anger at Jathbiyya was greater.

For Muhammad had set himself up as a rival for me long ago. The more I stewed, the more signs I remembered and recognized. His refusal to include me in outings with friends turned into exclusions in council. I went off to war and forgot about his pettiness. While I was away, he insinuated himself with our father, for the only purpose of ensuring he inherited. As I remembered these things, I realized that he had never really betrayed me—I had purposefully blinded myself to his nature, seeking to honor the precept of family over the machinations of court.

But Jathbiyya—the more I reflected on her, the more her corruption absolutely devastated me. I questioned everything, every kiss, every endearing comment. Was the entirety of our relationship a calculation to advance the interests of Byzantium?

After a year of fighting Byzantium, my empire was finally in peace. It was then that Ja'far approached me timidly. "Majesty?"

I sat on my throne, tired. My inner anger ate away at my energy, leaving me exhausted when not considering new acts of vengeance. "Yes?"

Ja'far shifted from foot to foot, nervous. "I-I conducted an investigation to get you answers—answers I think your heart needs. I have recovered documents from your late brother and wife's estates."

I shrugged. "They were liars and cheats. What else is new?"

Ja'far shifted uncomfortably. "Well, they certainly lacked a sense of morality, but there—there is more, Majesty."

"Just tell me."

"Well, it seems as though, in the end, Muhammad spoke the truth." Ja'far fumbled in a sack and removed a scrap of parchment. "Here is a letter from her. It instructs him on how to proceed. According to the dates on it, she sent it on long before the conversation with you about making him the heir."

Ja'far held out the parchment, but I waved my hand at it. He let it fall to the table next to me. Digging through his bag again, he removed a journal. "I also spoke with Lady—"

"Don't call her that."

He sighed. "With Jathbiyya's maid. Majesty, she was regularly taking cohosh and other herbs meant to prevent pregnancy."

The full implication of what Ja'far said settled on me.

I stood. "You mean to tell me that my wife avoided pregnancy to trick me into a situation where I would have to choose between her and the empire?"

Ja'far shook his head. "I mean that she was a plant from Byzantium sent to destabilize the empire, cause the throne to pass, by whatever means, to your battle-inexperienced brother, thus making our empire ripe for picking."

The magnitude of her duplicity smothered me. She had never loved me. She had never wanted to tie her life to mine. Everything, even her pleas in the dungeon, had all been a calculated lie to twist and maneuver me.

A tingling feeling started in my chest. It was as though my heart froze into a solid lump. The coldness, bitter, sharp, poison pulsed through my veins, freezing me from the inside out. Some part of me recognized that this feeling, this icy shock, was dangerous and should be stopped. But like mint, the initial bitterness turned sweet as I surrendered to its intoxicating pull.

"Fetch me the legislative code," I crooned to Ja'far.

He stepped back, eyes wide in fear. "Majesty?"

"The book. *Now.*"

And I wrote on a page of parchment:

> From this day forward, fully aware of the duplicitous, scheming, untrustworthy, and self-serving nature of woman, I, Shahryar al-Amin, decree thus: I will wed a new bride every night, and then, before she can use her womanly cunning to inflict harm on this Empire, execute her the following morning.

Signing and sealing it, I handed the book to Ja'far. He read it and paled. "Majesty—what is this? Do you really intend—"

"I will wait on it for three days. To consider. As you have requested I do for all new laws." I stared him down. "And then you will find me the brides I require."

"Now you know the truth, Sutaita. Do with it as you will." I left her in the gardens.

I couldn't bear to look at her. The pain of Jathbiyya's betrayal felt as if it happened yesterday.

One Thousand and One Days

Chapter 24
Day 1001: Sufaifa

The sun rose on the one thousand and first day of my marriage. I was out of time. Out of stories. And I knew enough about Shahryar now to know that when he realized I'd deceived him...

A lump formed in my throat. I was going to die today.

I noticed my husband stirring. He smiled at me as his eyes opened. His hand sought mine, and upon finding it, squeezed tightly. I struggled to keep my voice soft and my face kind. When would the killing blow come?

"Good morning, my lord. How did you sleep?"

His lips parted, revealing white teeth smiling against the darkness of his beard. "For the first time in over a thousand nights, I slept like an infant."

My heart beat harder in my chest. Despite our time together, despite the months of nights sharing stories, poetry, and even dreams, I still could not read him. Did he still plan to kill me? Had he finally found peace with his decision?

He leaned over and kissed my brow. "My beautiful wife—let us go and pray the morning prayers."

In the hallway outside the chamber, he turned to me. Lifting a hand, he stroked my cheek softly, his thumb caressing. I leaned into the caress. Dropping his hand, he turned to the right and entered his dressing room.

In my private dressing room, my maids assisted me with the daily bathing and ritual cleansing. I then joined my husband in the prayer nook. As one, we procured our prayer rugs, laid them out facing Mecca, and began the morning prayers. This shared faith had become the deepest expression of intimacy.

Afterward, we sat at an outdoor table tucked into a niche in the garden. The table had already been prepared with an assortment of food. I quietly served my husband, putting his favorite smoked meats on a plate, then handing it to him. I served myself a plate, but I felt too anxious to eat.

"So what story will you tell me tonight, Scheherazade?"

I looked up. He still used my father's nickname for me. Part of me wished I had never told him about that. I hoped—and feared—that it was love. I had been honest, perfectly honest with him for over a thousand days and nights. Now I must be honest this last time. A thousand fears and dreams rushed through me. Maybe he had changed. Maybe he would spare my life.

Maybe...just maybe...he loved me.

"My lord, I fear that I have no more stories to tell."

His face became like a stone.

There. It was out. I had said it. He would condemn or exonerate me as he desired. But my confession did not bring the relief I had hoped it would. I thought that admitting the truth would free me, release me from the fear I had lived with for years now. But it did not. No matter that I had eluded my fated death for a thousand and one nights. The time for reckoning was now upon me, and I was no more ready to die today than I had been the night of my marriage. And now, what to do? As I sat there, watching his face revert to the old, stony lines I thought I had eradicated from his face, I remembered Dunyazade's worry. I ran out of stories...I was supposed to have thought up a plan. I was supposed to have done something. After almost three years, I still had nothing.

The silence stretched around us. The rushing water of the fountains seemed to roar, filling the desolate space between us.

"Sutaita, I...am surprised by your announcement."

I swallowed. Here it was. My death sentence must be on his lips.

"I have some grave news to tell you." He turned from me and stared out over the garden.

Did his mind recall the hundreds of meals taken here? The walks, the discussions? Was he even now trying to decide how to tell me that I must be executed? My heart sank. He certainly was. Despite everything—the years, the time—he could never move past his trauma. I had started to wonder if maybe—but no. It was impossible.

The seconds stretched on. I stood waiting; my thudding heart made it feel like hours.

He finally turned from the fountain and met my eyes. "I owe you an apology."

"My lord, I—"

"Please." He walked back to me and took both my hands in his. "Please, hear me out, dear Scheherazade."

I tightened my lips, fighting tears. How could he be so tender when, moments ago, he was surely entertaining the thought of my death?

"I owe you an apology. Your revelation...caught me off guard." His lips turned up in a wry smile, his soft-brown eyes twinkling. "You and your stories...I was so swept up in them that I...well, I forgot."

"Forgot what, my lord?"

He sighed, a trace of sorrow returning to his eyes. "I forgot the how of our situation. I cannot even imagine what you must think of me..." He groaned in pain, dropping my hands and turning around to gaze into the fountain again. "You must have thought I was preparing to kill you."

My breath caught. He knew. Despite my care with my face, my emotions...he had slipped past my defenses and could read me like a book. Not daring to say anything, I chose silence as the best option.

He turned back to me, studying my face. He smiled a little to himself. "Of course. For, despite nearly three years together, I have never once done anything to assure you of..." He hesitated, as if afraid to finish. "Of my love for you, dear Scherezade."

The world seemed to stop spinning. He loved me? After the fights, the anger, the violence, everything—he loved me?

His gaze penetrated mine, searing my soul. I felt the words on my lips, the return of affection for him—but something stopped me from saying it. Something in me knew that, once said, those words would seal my fate. I would be inextricably linked to him forever, despite my dreams, my hopes...despite everything.

I sat there, unable to speak.

Sorrow consumed his eyes. "I do love you. I just—I hope you can forgive me. I hope you can love me as I love you."

And oh, how I wanted to forgive everything. I wanted to erase the memories of rough hands, hurtful words, distrustful gazes. I wanted to look at him and see only the shining self he presented in court, gilt with gold and presented as the sultan, representing the interests of Allah in his kingdom.

"Shahryar—I want to love you—I want to be swept up in this moment and forget everything except the warmth of your arms and the softness of your lips. But—"

"But what?" He rose and pulled me in close.

The scent of his ylang-ylang oil filled my head, and a voice inside begged me to abandon my concerns and give in. *Some things are as they are—let go and be happy with him. He loves you.*

And that was just the problem. I did love him back, no matter what. How could I love someone so evil, so morally bankrupt, that he would slaughter dozens of innocent women? That I had beguiled into loving me. And now that the veil had well and truly been drawn, what if he looked on me without covering, without artifice, and realized that, at my core, I was also merely a woman?

"I'm afraid. Oh, Shahryar, I'm afraid of the future. What if you change your mind? What if—"

He pulled me close, nestling my head on his shoulder. "I won't. I swear it. I love you, Sutaita. What I feel for you will never change."

I pushed away. He let go, hurt.

"You promised Jathbiyya the same thing. You promised her eternal love—and you killed her." I whirled away from him.

"Sutai—Scheherazade."

I squeezed my eyes shut when he called me by that nickname.

"Please. I am a changed man." He halted for a moment. "Come with me. Please?"

Was it possible for your heart to burst? Could a single person desire two such disparate things as marriage and solitude, partnership and independence? It was as if I existed in two separate places, with two separate identities: The married woman, the woman who had vowed her life to the man next to her, screamed for me to return his affection, to return his embrace, profess my love for him, and surrender myself completely to him. The independent woman, the woman who sought to further science and understanding, to make her own person of herself, unfettered by any commitments to others, begged me to turn away, to leave now.

Something wouldn't let me. I don't know if it was the earnest pleading in his eyes, the memory of passionate kisses, the promise of something more, something deeper, in the future, or the fruit of knowledge that always called to me. Heaven help me, I agreed to follow him at least one more time.

Chapter 25
Day 1001: Shahryar

I was a coward, a weakling who had given into anger. And now, my weakness threatened my happiness. For I loved Sutaita. Khaizuran had explained how Sutaita had decided upon stories. Her explanation was what decided me. I led her down the corridor to the archives.

When we approached, her steps slowed, and she looked at me, brows raised in question.

I laid her hand on my arm and continued on. "I should have told you weeks ago."

"Told me what?"

Rather than answer, I led her into the archives and headed toward the section that housed legislative codes. I removed the last book on the shelf and opened it to the last page. "Here. See for yourself."

She reached out to take the book, eyes immediately drawn to the text. My lovely scholar, already immersed in knowledge. Her eyes widened in shock. "When? Why?"

"Over a month ago. I meant to tell you. I was just—"

"Scared." Her gaze softened.

"Sutaita, I also need to tell you—I forgive you. I know that you plotted to use your stories to escape execution."

"M-my lord, I—"

I reached out a finger and laid it on her lips. "In a way, I am grateful that you did. You showed me that, while people may plot and scheme, sometimes it is for a greater good. You sought only to preserve your sister's life."

She tried to interrupt me, but I shook my head. "I have spent so much time reflecting on the past... How many days have we been married?"

"One thousand and one," she murmured.

"In the past one thousand and one days—days that I made very difficult for you. Remembering the tears and the difficulties, of how stalwart you were as I learned, finally, how to control my anger... There must have been days where death seemed preferable. And yet you soldiered on, and in doing so, have won more than just my love. You have gotten something I never gave to Jathbiyya—my respect and admiration. You have truly bewitched me, dearest Scherezade. You have set me free. And I love you more than anything in this wide world."

She stepped back and, after a moment, looked down at the floor, unable to meet my eyes. The depth of emotion shining from them overwhelmed me. Had we both just been too scared to admit this truth to each other the whole time?

She looked back into my face, her skin pale. "Shahryar—we have shared a wonderful, terrifying, elating, and earth-shattering thousand and one days together. I do love you, more than I ever thought it possible to love anyone. But—"

With that one word, my heart ripped apart. I had feared as much—she would never be able to forgive my bloody past. Despite my love, despite my honesty, it was too much, even for someone as understanding and intelligent as Sutaita.

"But what?" Would she tell me? Or would she resume the pattern of betrayal for trust, disdain for love? I would have to listen.

I realized that listening was my problem. Had I listened to others, actually listened to Jathbiyya, instead of drowning in her dazzling smile, I would have seen the truth she sought to hide from me. It wasn't until Sutaita, and night after night of glorious stories, that I began to understand just how important listening was.

Sutaita bit her lip. "But I need freedom. I need the chance to actually make a choice for me—not for family, for convention, or even for you—the man I love."

I looked at her—for what was probably the first time, I actually looked at the woman I professed to love. She had bowed her head, crying.

Something else pulled at me: choice. She had actually listened to my stories—listened not to condemn me, but to understand me. And in doing so, she understood me, at this moment, better than I understood myself. Jathbiyya certainly hadn't chosen me. None of the women I'd married had ever chosen me.

With the exception of my father on his deathbed, no one had ever chosen me for myself. Even my father had resigned to the realization that I was a better choice—not that he loved me more or wished for me to have the experience of being Sultan. And as I chewed over Sutaita's words, I realized the depth of love she truly had for me.

Scherezade—freedom. An idea that, for her whole life, had been a fantasy she was named. If I loved her, if I truly loved her for who she was, and the person she sought to become, how could I do anything less? I had to give her everything—to do any less would invalidate the love I claimed to have.

That decided me. I reached out and tilted her face up. Sutaita's eyes were red-rimmed and swollen, her cheeks streaked with salty tears. This would not do. I wanted to see the one thing I had not seen in a thousand and one days of knowing this woman: her smile. I used my thumb to brush a droplet away from her eye. Though it would almost kill me to do it, I needed to grant her request.

"My dear Scherezade. Just as soon as I think I understand you, you show me again how much I underestimate you." I pulled her into me, to give her one last hug, to feel her warmth and beauty and wonder cleave to me one last time. "I will always love you, my dearest, dearest Scherezade. And if I love you as ardently and truly as I profess, then the only thing I could possibly do would be to set you free."

Sutaita gaped at me. Her eyes were open so wide, I could see the pearly whites all around the edges of the bloom of the iris. "Come again?"

"I love you. I will always love you. All I want is your happiness." As I spoke these words, the full truth dawned on me. "I—I think I finally understand it. If I keep you, force you to stay with me against your will, deny you the one thing your heart and soul need, how am I any better than Jathbiyya or Muhammad?"

And I made peace with the last part of me that succumbed to rage. Their betrayal and choices had nothing to do with me. I had been right to make the choices I had. The suffering of civil war, and the later war with Byzantium, were not a reflection on me. From now on, I would need to choose the path of honesty and love. I would need to become who I was before. Part of me would always wonder at potential schemes and intrigues—which was necessary to be a ruler. But from this day forth, I would seek justice instead of vengeance. I would strive to be fair, not vindictive.

"You will have all the freedom I can grant you. I promise."

Finally, after a thousand and one days, her lips curved and parted, framing ivory teeth while lighting up her eyes like stars in the night sky. It was more beautiful than anything I had ever seen.

She smiled and looked back down at the book, where the reversal of my edict was codified into law. "Since you give me freedom, I return it. I give you freedom from the past." With that, she shut the book and returned it to the shelf. "That was then. Now, this person in front of me, this man who was swept away by tales, who always seeks to do the right thing, who wants a simple love, not a kingly love—that is the man I love."

Here she offered me the gift I had yearned for all my life: truly unconditional and undying love. No limits, no reasons, no expectations.

I grabbed her close and kissed her, a kiss she returned with the undying passion she professed mere moments ago.

Acknowledgments

I wanted to take a short moment to thank all the people who helped bring this to publication and share some of my research for anyone who wants to learn more about the Abbasid Caliphate, the inspiration for this retelling.

First and foremost, thanks to my late father, Jamie Donald, who was my first alpha reader, and the most encouraging person in my life, after my husband. I also want to thank my amazing business partners, Brandi Spencer and Rebecca Mikkelson, who have been by my side every step of the way. Finally, I want to thank my sensitivity and cultural readers, Gabriel Stevenson and Noreen Lekhak, who gave me invaluable insight into the nuances of the culture, the Islam religion, and how to portray both in an authentic and honorable way.

The inspiration for this story came from a prompt to write a fairy tale with a twist. Sutaita is based on Sutayta al Mahmali, a female Muslim mathematician from the 10th century. Shahryar is based on Al-Ma'mun, son of Harun al Rashid, and Muhammad is based on the same's brother. Although most people link the father, Harun, with the Arabian Nights story, the succession wars following Harun's death were more interesting to me.

If you enjoyed the story, and want to learn more, look up the Golden Age of Islam, the House of Wisdom (which was real), and the Abbasid dynasty.

Also by Renee Frey

"Jump Discontinuity"
"The Princess and the Frog"

About the Author

Renee has been published in two anthologies and is currently working on two standalone novels with two series in pre-development. She enjoys reading and writing fantasy for both adults and young adults. She lives in Pennsylvania with her husband, Mike, and their two dogs: a puggle named Ziggy and a chihuahua named Megatron. Renee graduated Summa Cum Laude from West Chester University with a BA in English Literature. When she is not writing, she makes her living in instructional design, technical writing, and teaching dance.

Follow her online:

ReneeFreyAuthor.com
Facebook: @renee.frey.18007
Twitter: @ReneeFreyAuthor

Authors 4 Authors
Publishing

A publishing company for authors, run by authors, blending the best of traditional and independent publishing

We specialize in speculative fiction: science fiction, fantasy, paranormal, and romance. Get lost in another world!

Check out our collection at https://books2read.com/rl/a4a or visit Authors4AuthorsPublishing.com/books

For updates, scan the QR code or visit our website to join our semi-monthly newsletter!

Want more romance? We recommend:

FYR
by Lisa Borne Graves

At seventeen, Toury arrives in Fyr, where magic is power, a prince's love is deadly, and female autonomy is a dream. Alex, the Prince of Fyr, has to face his father's ailing health, the expectation to marry soon, and the hidden necromancers trying to take over the realm by exploiting his dark curse. At least there's hope in a cheeky savior, but Earth girls aren't so easy. Can they trust each other enough to save Fyr? Or will everything they hold dear turn to ash?

books2read.com/fyr

www.ingramcontent.com/pod-product-compliance
Lightning Source LLC
Chambersburg PA
CBHW020330110726
47898CB00003B/816